Betrayal

Center Point
Large Print

Also by Robin Lee Hatcher and available from Center Point Large Print:

Where the Heart Lives Series
Belonging

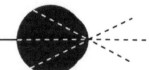

**This Large Print Book carries the
Seal of Approval of N.A.V.H.**

Betrayal

WHERE THE HEART LIVES

ROBIN LEE HATCHER

CENTER POINT LARGE PRINT
THORNDIKE, MAINE

This Center Point Large Print edition is published in the year 2013 by arrangement with Zondervan.

All Scripture quotations, unless otherwise noted, are taken from the King James Version.

The text of this Large Print edition is unabridged. In other aspects, this book may vary from the original edition. Printed in the United States of America on permanent paper. Set in 16-point Times New Roman type.

ISBN: 978-1-61173-601-4

Library of Congress Cataloging-in-Publication Data

Hatcher, Robin Lee.
Betrayal / Robin Lee Hatcher.
pages ; cm.
ISBN 978-1-61173-601-4 (library binding : alk. paper)
1. Ranch life—Wyoming—Fiction. 2. Large type books. I. Title.
PS3558.A73574B48 2013
813′.54—dc23
2012035556

And those who know Your name
will put their trust in You,
For You, O LORD, have not forsaken
those who seek You.

Psalm 9:10 NASB

Betrayal

Prologue

Spring 1881

The train belched black smoke as it chugged across the wide prairie. In the third railcar were twenty-six orphans and two adults from Dr. Cray's Asylum for Little Wanderers. The children had left Chicago and were headed west for placement, hoping to leave poverty, cold, and hunger behind them.

Technically, the Brennan children weren't orphans. Although their mother had died this past winter, their father was still alive. Somewhere. Least as far as anyone knew. But when it came to his children, Sweeney Brennan was as good as dead.

Thirteen-year-old Hugh was now the head of the family. He'd promised his mother on her deathbed that he would take care of his younger sisters. He was determined to keep that promise. Only how? He'd been warned it was unlikely they would find a family to take in all three. Well, he would just have to do some fast talking. If he'd inherited anything from his father, it was the gift of gab.

Hugh turned away from the window to look at his sisters. Leaning against each other, Felicia and

9

Diana slept, lulled by the warmth of the railcar. Wisps of Felicia's long hair fell across her face. He leaned forward and brushed it aside.

She opened her eyes and gave him a groggy look. "Are we there?" she whispered.

"Not yet. Soon, I think."

Releasing a sigh, she closed her eyes again.

I'll take care of them, Mum. I won't fail you. You'll see.

One

May 1899

Julia Grace shielded her eyes against the sun as she stood on the bluff and stared south. Far in the distance, a train churned its way west across the plains, a ribbon of smoke trailing from its stack. As always, she wondered about the passengers onboard. What was their destination? Was someone waiting for them once they arrived, or were they all alone in the world? Alone . . . like her.

A warm wind whistled around her, tugging on her skirt, pulling her hair free from its ribbon. Spring had arrived in Wyoming at last, kissing the mountains and plains with green. The highest peaks were still white with snow, but down below, a harsh winter was forgotten. New life was everywhere, from the shoots of grass in the forest meadows to the leaves unfurling on trees to the baby hawks in the rocky crag overlooking Burt's Canyon to the calves cavorting in the pastures.

She hated the harsh Wyoming winters—had hated them ever since she'd come here as a new bride. Most years it seemed that the cold, snowy, dark season would never end. But spring inevitably came—and with it, Julia's freedom. Freedom to roam. Freedom to ride. Freedom to dream. Freedom to escape the pain, both physical and emotional.

Only, she didn't need to escape now. She *was* free. Really free.

Teddy, her black gelding, nickered.

Julia turned around. "Taking too long, am I?"

The horse bobbed his head.

She laughed. If her brother-in-law were to hear her talking to Teddy, he would declare her insane. Come to think of it, he'd probably like that. It would give him control of the ranch, and he wouldn't even have to convince her to sell.

She drew a deep breath and forced the unpleasant thoughts from her mind. She wasn't going to let her husband's half-brother spoil this beautiful day for her. She knew she would be forced to deal with him again. But not right now.

Julia stepped to Teddy's side and swung into the saddle. By the time she'd collected the reins in one hand, she saw Bandit, her spaniel, racing toward her, bounding over the sagebrush, long tongue flapping out one side of his mouth like a flag.

Laughter bubbled up again. Maybe she *was* daft, but she didn't care. Sadness and fear had stalked her for too many years. She was tired of it. She refused to allow its return. Rejoice, the Good Book said. Rejoice in every circumstance. She meant to put those words into practice.

She turned Teddy away from the bluff and nudged him into a canter, riding toward the small ranch she'd named Sage-hen. Angus Grace, her husband of eleven years, had mocked her because of the name. Land was land, he'd said. It didn't need a name. But with Angus's death thirteen months ago, Sage-hen had become hers, and she would call it what she pleased. She'd paid for that right in countless ways, including in her own blood.

Dusk shrouded the earth by the time Hugh Brennan decided to make camp for the night. After taking care of the horse, he built a fire and warmed a can of beans over it. Not much of a supper, but he'd eaten worse. He'd even gone without food plenty of nights, so he wouldn't complain.

If he was right about how far he'd traveled this week, he should cross over into Idaho by late tomorrow afternoon. Maybe another week or ten days and he would reach the capital city. Of course, if he had the money for train fare, he would be there already, but he was dead broke. Work was hard to come by. Strange, the way people looked at him and seemed to know his history.

With his belly full, he lay on his back and stared at the stars. There'd been plenty of times when he couldn't see the sky, day or night, and he didn't fail to be thankful that he could see it now. It made the night spent on the hard ground seem not as long.

Years ago, Hugh had told his sister Felicia that as long as she could see the Big Dipper she would know they weren't far apart, that he would be looking up at the very same constellation and thinking of her and Diana, that he would find his sisters again. He'd been a boy of thirteen when he'd uttered those words of assurance. He was no longer a boy. Eighteen years had come and gone without him keeping his promise. But another week, maybe two, and he might find Felicia at last. Would she be glad to see him? Or had too much time passed for her to care?

Maybe. Maybe not. But he had to try. He owed it to his mother's memory if nothing else.

Felicia Kristoffersen. That's the name his sister went by now. She'd taken the last name of the people who'd raised her. Had they been good to her? Had they loved her? He had his doubts, judging by the so-called relatives he'd met on the farm in eastern Wyoming.

Eighteen years. Maybe it was unrealistic to try to find her after so long. She must have a new and better life. What would she need with a brother like him, coming around to spoil things for her?

Eighteen years. He closed his eyes, trying to shut out the memories that threatened. Trying not to smell the stink of a tenement flat. Trying not to imagine himself slipping through a narrow opening into a darkened house that wasn't his own. Trying not to hear the slurred speech of his father, the slamming of iron doors, the harsh orders of guards. Trying not to feel the blows that fell like rain, fist against flesh.

Trying but failing.

This would be another night of bad dreams.

Two

The chickens scolded as Julia took fresh eggs from the nests inside the coop. She paid them no heed; the sound was as familiar to her ears as the sight of the sun rising in the east each morning was to her eyes. Beyond the wire that enclosed the coop, protecting the birds from predators, Bandit lay in the barnyard, head upon his paws, waiting for Julia to finish her morning chores.

Dear Bandit. He'd been her faithful friend through thick and thin these past nine years. He wasn't as fast as he'd once been, and she suspected his eyes weren't as sharp either. But his heart was as big as ever. Oh, that more people could love as deeply as her brown and white spaniel.

"Ready for breakfast?" she asked the dog as she unlatched the gate and stepped out of the enclosure.

Bandit was instantly on his feet, expectation in his dark eyes. Julia would swear he smiled at her.

"Of course you are." She laughed softly as she turned toward the house.

Bandit ran ahead of her, but before he reached the porch, he stopped and stared off to the south. His head lowered, and he growled a warning. Julia turned in the direction of the dog's gaze in time to see a lone man leave the trees, leading his horse. Alarm shot through her. She'd left the rifle inside the house, something she rarely did since the death of her husband. It was always better to be prepared for trouble. If not from men, then from bears or rattlers.

"Easy, Bandit," she said softly, moving toward the dog without taking her eyes off the man.

He was a stranger to her. She could see that as he drew closer. He had a handsome face, despite a pale scar on his right cheek, a noticeable zigzag that cut into the dark shadow of a beard on his jaw. Lines etched the corners of his eyes and his mouth. She guessed him to be a few years her senior. No more than thirty-five.

He stopped a short distance away. "Ma'am." He tugged the brim of his hat. "My horse pulled up lame a ways back and could use some rest. Could we trouble you for a drink of water?"

She nodded, then motioned with her head toward the pump. "Help yourself."

Bandit sat and continued to watch the man while his mistress carried the basket of eggs into the house. On her way back to the porch, Julia picked up her rifle and moved it to a spot just outside the door. She wanted the stranger to know she wasn't vulnerable. In fact, she'd become a good shot, as long as her target wasn't moving too fast.

After the man—now hatless—slaked his thirst from the stream flowing out of the spout, he filled his canteen and then splashed water on his face and the back of his neck. He finished by slicking his thick dark hair with both hands as he straightened, his gaze moving toward the house.

"I'm obliged." Motioning to the horse drinking from the trough, he added, "Both of us are."

She nodded.

"How far am I from the nearest town?"

"A couple hours' ride. Less if you push your horse."

The man squinted toward the west. "Can't push him. Guess it'll take longer."

He looked hungry. Not that his stomach was any of her concern.

"You wouldn't be looking for a hired hand, would you?"

She didn't answer.

"Temporary. Just until my horse heals up?" The stranger picked up his hat and set it over his dampened hair.

Julia didn't want anyone to work for her. Couldn't afford to hire a hand for one thing. Liked her solitude for another. Still, the fellow *did* look hungry, and his horse *was* favoring his left foreleg. Against her better judgment, she said, "I reckon I might need a few things done around the place. Until your horse is healed. Can't pay you anything, but you'll have plenty to eat while you're here."

Relief flashed in his eyes.

"You look as if you could use some grub now."

Relief changed to surprise. "Yes, ma'am."

She supposed he couldn't be any more surprised by her offer than she was. "Turn your horse into the corral there. It won't take me long to whip up some breakfast."

"That's kind of you."

She shrugged as she turned and went inside.

What on earth was she thinking? Offering a drifter breakfast and a job, no matter how tempo-rary. How did she know he wasn't dangerous? It wasn't as if Sage-hen was on a well-traveled road.

It was a good piece off the beaten path. What was he doing in these parts? Then again, he didn't look like a thief so much as someone who'd fallen on hard times. From the look of his shaggy hair, he hadn't been near a barber in a couple of months.

"That's kind of you."

He wasn't from around these parts. That was clear in his voice. He had a slight accent of some sort, although she wasn't well-traveled enough to recognize where from. Then again, it didn't much matter where he was from or where he was going. She'd promised him breakfast, and she'd best get him fed.

Before long, strips of bacon sizzled in the skillet while Julia sliced and buttered bread that she'd baked the previous day. Next she fried half a dozen eggs in the bacon drippings. It wasn't until she was moving the eggs from frying pan to plate that she heard the sound of chopping coming from outside. The stranger's plate in her hands, she moved to the open door.

Hugh brought the ax down with force, splitting the wood in two, sending small chips flying. There was something satisfying about chopping fire-wood. He supposed it was because he could see the results of his labor as the stack of fresh-cut pieces grew.

"Mister. Your breakfast is growing cold."

He turned toward the house. The woman stood

on the porch, a plate in her right hand, the other hand on her hip. Behind her was the rifle she'd placed there as an obvious warning. He guessed that meant she was here alone. Was her man away or dead? Had to be one or the other. He couldn't imagine she'd go unmarried in a land where women were always in the minority. Especially one this pretty.

Hugh put down the ax, leaning it against the tree stump that served as a chopping block. Then he strode toward her and the promised breakfast. As he drew closer and caught that first scent of bacon, his stomach growled.

The hint of a smile curved her mouth as she held the plate toward him. "You can eat out here on the porch."

"I appreciate it, ma'am."

"My name is Julia Grace."

"Hugh Brennan, ma'am." He took the plate from her hand. "I appreciate it, Mrs. Grace."

She neither confirmed nor denied the existence of a Mr. Grace.

Hugh sank onto the top step of the porch and began to eat. He forced himself to take his time, to savor the food. She'd agreed to let him stay and work for her while his horse rested his bad leg, but she might still change her mind. He could be eating beans two or three times a day in the blink of an eye.

"Thanks for chopping the wood," she said from

19

the doorway. Before he could respond, soft foot steps told him she'd gone inside.

Hugh gave his full attention to the eggs, bacon, and buttered bread. Despite the watchful eyes of the dog who seemed to be guarding him, he enjoyed every bite, wiping up the crumbs and egg yolk from the tin plate with the last bit of bread before popping it into his mouth.

His hunger sated, he let his gaze sweep the barnyard and outbuildings. Nothing about the place said prosperity. A better description was sturdy and solid. The house and outbuildings had been made to withstand the harsh Rocky Mountain winters. Not that he knew anything about farms or ranches. Except for a brief spell in Nebraska, he'd spent his entire life in the city or in—

He broke off the thought. " 'Therefore,' " he whispered, " 'if any man be in Christ, he is a new creature: old things are passed away; behold, all things are become new.' "

He looked toward the woodpile and decided to finish chopping the logs that were there. He would make certain Julia Grace had no reason to regret her charity. There was no law that said she had to feed a hungry stranger or give him a place to lay his head at night—unless one counted what it said about such things in the Bible. And it had been Hugh's experience that even those who gave credence to the Scriptures didn't always do

.vhat it said in that regard. He'd slept on the hard ground and had an empty belly often enough to prove it.

Releasing a long breath, he set the plate on the stoop and got to his feet. The spaniel stood too.

"Relax."

The dog gave a low growl.

Hugh raised his hands in a sign of surrender. "It's all right, you mangy hound. I'm just after another drink of water."

"You insult Bandit, Mr. Brennan. He's never had mange."

He turned toward the entrance to the house again. "Sorry. No insult intended. But I don't think your dog likes me."

"He has good reason to distrust men."

There was something in the way she said the words, a particular inflection in her voice, that made him wonder if the same could be said of her.

She bent down to retrieve his plate. "Did you get enough to eat?"

"Yes'm, I did. Thanks." He gestured with his thumb. "I thought I'd split the rest of that wood. Unless there's something else you'd like me to do."

"No. The wood's fine." She paused for a moment, then added, "You'll find your quarters at the back of the barn. Let me know if there's something you need that's not there. It's been awhile since I had a hired man on the place."

21

"I'm sure it'll be fine, Mrs. Grace."

She gave him an abrupt nod before turning and disappearing once again inside the house.

Experience had taught Hugh how to read most people, but Julia Grace was proving a bit harder to figure out than most. She had her guard up, and she was good at concealing her emotions. Not that he could blame her. She had no reason to trust him farther than she could throw him—which wouldn't be far at all, slight as she was.

With a shake of his head, he strode to the chopping block, picked up the ax, and set to work.

Despite questioning the wisdom of allowing Hugh Brennan to stay, Julia couldn't help but be thankful for his help with the firewood. It was one of the few chores she truly detested. And she'd learned the hard way how important it was to chop as much firewood as possible while the weather was warm so there would be plenty to be had after winter set in.

Watching him through the window, she noted how easy he made the task look. He'd rolled up the sleeves of his shirt, revealing strong biceps. He worked in an easy rhythm—set the log on the stump, step back, swing the ax back and around and down, pick up the split wood, set the pieces on the stack, grab another log, do it all over again.

He hadn't asked for more than what she'd offered. Still, she wished she could pay him for his labor. Something more than food in his belly and a bunk in the barn. Unfortunately, she had no money to spare. Wouldn't have any until she culled the herd later in the month, and even then the money she received from the sale would most likely be just enough to see her through the next year. That's how it was for most ranchers. Only cattle barons—and there were few enough of them—had the luxury of plenty of cash in their pockets. Most of the rest lived hand-to-mouth.

Turning her back to the window, Julia wondered if Angus had ever worried he might lose Sage-hen after a harsh winter or when the price of beef on the hoof wasn't as high as expected. Not that her husband would have told her. He hadn't thought the day-to-day operation of the ranch any of her business. And if he'd known he was going to die, he wouldn't have left Sage-hen to his wife either.

The knowledge stung her heart, but not as much as it once had.

Hugh awakened with a start, heart hammering. Sometimes, the nightmares lingered, vivid and precise in every way. Other times all he remembered was being afraid but not knowing why. He could never decide if one kind was better than the other.

He tossed the blanket aside and rose from the bed, pulling on his shirt before he'd straightened to his full height. The room held a cot, a small table, and two wooden chairs, and wasn't much larger than one of the stalls in the barn—or a prison cell. Three strides took him to the door. Not many more carried him outside.

Light from the full moon threw a blanket of white over the barnyard, chicken coop, corral, and house. Leaning a shoulder against the corner of the barn, he wondered again about the widow woman who'd given him shelter. She didn't seem the type to live alone on a remote spread like this. There was a delicacy about her that seemed at odds with the rugged land where she lived. It made him want to know her story, which surprised him. Hugh rarely asked questions about others because it invited them to ask questions about him. Better to keep to himself.

He turned his back to the wall of the barn, leaned against it, and closed his eyes. Then he waited. Waited for the last dregs of the nightmare to fade away. Waited to forget the man he used to be. Waited for the fragile peace he'd found in a Savior to sweep over him, even though he didn't fully understand that Savior yet. Waited.

He was good at waiting. It was a trait he'd learned in prison. If he hadn't learned it, the cramped space he'd lived in for so many years would have driven him mad.

The click of Bandit's claws on the floor awakened Julia. The dog paced from the bedroom

24

to the front door and back to the bedroom again.

"Do you need out, boy?"

Bandit whimpered his affirmation.

"All right." She pushed aside the blanket and got up. "I'm coming." Her way was illuminated by moonlight coming through the windows.

The instant the front door opened, Bandit shot through it, racing out to relieve himself. Julia started to close the door, but then she saw him—Hugh Brennan, his back against the barn, standing in the moonlight. Bandit saw him too, but the dog didn't raise an alarm. He simply moved toward Hugh, alert but not concerned. Apparently the spaniel had accepted the newcomer. That was good to know. Julia had learned to put stock in Bandit's opinion of people; he'd proven himself a good judge of character.

Where had Hugh been headed, she wondered, before he stopped at Sage-hen to ask for a drink of water and a respite for his horse? Where had he come from? She supposed it showed an alarming lack of curiosity—if not some more serious flaw in her character—that she wanted to know little other than his name. But why should she want to know more? He wouldn't be here long. A few days of rest, and then he would move on. Whatever his previous destination had been, that's where he would go, and she would never see him again.

Which was fine with her.

She continued to watch him, wondering what held his gaze. Perhaps it was the moon. Or perhaps he watched the treetops as they swayed in the night breeze. Or perhaps his eyes had been closed this entire time.

But then Hugh noticed Bandit. The man pushed away from the barn and spoke softly to the dog, at the same time appearing to look toward the house. Could he see her? She didn't think so. But he must have known she was there all the same. Squatting, he held out his hand. Bandit went closer but stayed just out of reach; the dog might have accepted the man's presence, but they weren't friends yet. As Julia had told Hugh earlier, Bandit had plenty of reasons to distrust men.

As did she.

An unpleasant memory from a night much like this one—moonlight flooding the barnyard, the air crisp but not cold—suddenly overtook her. She heard her husband's angry voice and Bandit's painful yelp, felt the thudding of her heart, steeled herself against whatever might come next.

"What a pitiful excuse for a woman you are."

The words, echoing from the past, left a hollow sensation in their wake. Tears slipped from her eyes to track her cheeks, but she swept them away with her fingertips. She wanted to be done with tears. It was time to be done with the pain.

She left the door ajar for Bandit and returned

to her bedroom where she crawled beneath the covers and lay staring at the ceiling. Sleep wouldn't come again, but she would lie there anyway and wait out the night.

Hugh had known she was there in the doorway, watching him, watching the dog. Her white nightgown had given her away, despite how she'd kept to the shadows of the house. Was she afraid of him? Maybe, but she hadn't let that stop her from helping him. It took courage to act despite one's fears, and he'd learned to appreciate courage, when a person did what was right, no matter the opposition. Instinct told Hugh that Julia Grace had faced more than her fair share of opposition.

Julia Grace.

The name seemed to fit her. Especially the last name. Grace. Simple elegance. Simple would describe the dark brown skirt and the light brown blouse she'd worn when he first saw her. Simple would describe the way she wore her honey-brown hair, captured neatly with a ribbon at the nape of her neck. And elegant would describe the arch of her brows above eyes of robin-egg blue and the delicacy of her pale, flawless skin.

Julia Grace.

It had been a long time since he'd allowed himself to give much notice to a female. Most women, leastwise the type he'd care to know, didn't want anything to do with a man like him. Maybe that's what she'd thought as she stood in the doorway awhile ago. That she didn't want anything to do with him. That she wished she hadn't given him a place to sleep. That she hoped he would pack up and move on.

Well, that's what he wanted too. To be on his way just as soon as possible.

Hugh returned to the sleeping quarters inside the barn. He struck a match and lit the oil lamp, throwing a golden glow over the room, and sat on one of the chairs. No point getting back into the bed. He wouldn't sleep. Might as well read. So he reached into the saddlebag hanging over the spindle of the other chair and withdrew the Bible from inside.

The book—the black leather cover worn, pages crinkled by time and use—had been given to Hugh by a preacher he'd met at Dr. Cray's when he went there to learn information about his sisters. At the time, he hadn't thought it would mean much of anything to him. He wasn't even sure why he'd kept it. But somewhere in Colorado, as he made his way west, that had changed. This Bible had become a lifeline, helping him discover who he was supposed to be, teaching him to look forward rather than back. Little by little, he'd learned there wasn't much in life that was under his control, not even outside of prison walls. And so he'd tried—was still trying—to give control of his life to the One who'd saved him from himself.

He opened the Bible to a now favorite chapter, Romans 12:

And be not conformed to this world: but be ye transformed by the renewing of your mind, that ye may prove what is that good, and acceptable, and perfect, will of God.

Prove what was the perfect will of God. He hadn't learned how to do that yet. It almost sounded easy here, the way the verse was written, but it wasn't easy.

Was he supposed to try to find his sisters? And even if the answer was yes, what was he to do with his life afterward? Plenty of folks wouldn't bother to give him work if they knew his past. Was he to keep it a secret, or was that the same as lying? How did he live out this new life with his renewed mind?

His mum used to say, when he wasn't sure what to do, to keep moving forward and eventually God would make things clear. He sure hoped she was right.

Three

At this time of the year, sunrise arrived at Sage-hen Ranch shortly after 5:00 a.m. On this particular morning, Julia was up, dressed, and outside as a pewter dawn spread across the barnyard. But before she reached the chicken coop, Hugh Brennan appeared in the barn doorway. He stopped when he saw her. She did the same.

"Morning, Mrs. Grace."

"Morning, Mr. Brennan. I hope you found the quarters comfortable."

"I did, ma'am." He motioned toward her basket. "Would you like me to gather the eggs for you?"

The offer surprised her. Angus would never have volunteered to go anywhere near the hen-house. Gathering eggs was woman's work, and he'd never allowed her to forget what her work was.

"Ma'am?"

She gave her head a slight shake. "No. Thank you, Mr. Brennan. I'll do it. I'll call you when breakfast is ready. But you could feed the horses in the corral, if you don't mind."

As Julia started forward, Bandit left her side and trotted over to Hugh. Unlike in the night, this time the dog didn't stop out of reach. He seemed to have made up his mind about the man. She hoped Hugh was deserving of Bandit's trust. And her own, guarded though it was.

It didn't take long to gather the eggs and return to the house. Breakfast was the same as the day before, only this time she scrambled the eggs and toasted the slices of buttered bread in the frying pan. When everything was ready, she went to the front porch and called for Hugh to join her before returning to the kitchen.

A short while later, he arrived at the open door. "Are you sure, Mrs. Grace?"

She didn't have to ask what he meant. Yesterday, she'd served him two meals, both times taking a plate to him outside. "I'm sure."

He stepped inside, lowering his head so as not to hit it on the doorjamb on his way through. She wondered, considering his height, if his feet hung off the end of the bunk in the barn. She thought they must have—and she found the image that popped into her mind disturbing.

"Smells good." He settled onto a chair at the table.

"There's not much damage a person can do to eggs and bacon. That's what my husband used to say." The instant the words were out of her mouth, she was sorry she'd said them. She didn't like to talk about Angus. Talking about him only served to bring up bad memories.

She took her place opposite Hugh, bowed her

head, and gave silent thanks for God's provision. When she looked up again, she saw that Hugh had bowed his head as well. Was he waiting for her to speak a blessing over the food? Just in case, she said, "Amen."

"Amen." He opened his eyes, tossed her a brief smile, and began to eat.

He wasn't much of a conversationalist. That was for certain. Normally, she wouldn't mind. She was comfortable with silence and her own thoughts. But she'd gotten an idea early this morning when she couldn't go back to sleep, and now she wanted to know more about the man seated across from her.

She picked up her fork. "Where do you come from, Mr. Brennan?"

"Illinois. My sisters and I were born in Chicago."

"Then you're a long way from home."

"Yes'm. I'm a long way."

"And where are you headed?"

"To Boise."

She waited, expecting him to elaborate, but he didn't. She decided to change tack. "How is your horse's leg this morning?"

"He's still favoring it. Can't tell why. I haven't found any sort of wound, and there's nothing in his hoof that I can see. Afraid I don't know much about doctoring animals."

"There's liniment in the tack room. That might help."

He nodded.

Julia set down her fork. She might as well get to the point. "Mr. Brennan, would it be a problem if you delayed your trip to Boise for a short while longer? A few weeks at most."

He cocked an eyebrow but said nothing.

"I'm going to need help driving my cattle to market, and the men who used to work for my husband have been hired on by another rancher. Besides, I can't offer much of a salary, and I couldn't give you any money until after the cattle are sold. But if you're interested, you'll eat good and you'll have a roof over your head at night. The way it is now. Would you be interested?"

Hugh seemed to ponder the offer, and Julia couldn't decide if she wanted him to accept or reject it. She still knew little about him and wasn't sure why she'd felt compelled to ask him to work for her, other than because she needed the help and he seemed to like her cooking enough that he might not quibble over his pay.

At long last, he replied, "All right, Mrs. Grace. I don't suppose a few weeks more or less matters. Not where I'm going. I'll admit I wouldn't mind more of your good vittles. A man gets tired of beans day in and day out. But you should know, I've never done any ranch work. Green. Isn't that what you call it?"

Julia released the breath she hadn't known she held. "When my husband was alive, I wasn't involved with the everyday duties of running the ranch. I tended the home and Angus looked after the cattle. But since he died, I've been learning. If I can learn, so can you. Can you rope?"

A smile slipped into the corners of his mouth. "No, ma'am. Not much call for roping in the city."

Was he laughing at her? She bristled, and her feelings must have shown on her face.

He quickly sobered. "Why don't you tell me a little more about the place and what you're wanting me to do?"

Her irritation cooled. She was too sensitive, and she knew it. "Sage-hen isn't a large ranch. Less than two hundred acres. It's all fenced and the soil is rich. Irrigation from the river that runs through it allows enough forage to keep a couple hundred cows, each with a calf. I don't have that many. I had to sell more than I wanted last year after Angus passed on." She took a sip of coffee.

Hugh gave a brief nod, showing he listened.

"In the next week or two, I need to brand this year's calves. By the first of June, I'll have to drive the cattle I'm selling down to a ranch on the plains. It's not a long drive, and the two of us should be able to handle it without more help." They'd better be able to handle it. She couldn't afford to hire another hand, even an inexperienced one like Hugh Brennan. "Until then, you can make a few repairs around the place and help care for the livestock."

"I reckon I can at that." He took a few quick bites, cleaning the last of the food from his plate.

Normally, Julia was wary of men. Strangers in particular. But there was something about this man—

"Where would you like me to start, ma'am?"

"Perhaps you could start by calling me Julia. I'm afraid all your ma'ams are making me . . . I don't know . . . self-conscious."

His smile returned, and she noticed for the first time that it was slightly lopsided, lifting higher in the right corner of his mouth. Was it due to the pale scar on that cheek? Perhaps. But no matter the cause, the smile was appealing. Most women must find him attractive.

The heat of embarrassment rose in her cheeks. Lowering her gaze to her plate, she said, "Go ahead and tend to your horse. I'll be out to show you around after I'm done with the dishes."

Julia Grace was a strange one, Hugh thought as he worked the liniment into his gelding's leg. She couldn't seem to decide whether or not she should trust him. Or like him, for that matter. One moment she said to call her Julia because being called ma'am made her feel self-conscious; the next she dismissed him without a glance. Maybe that's what came of living alone out in the middle of nowhere without another soul to talk to.

People were meant to have relationships. That's what he'd heard a preacher in Nebraska say. That's what God intended. His people were meant to be in community, giving and sharing, praying and blessing. True enough, he supposed. But the risk of betrayal increased with close connections to others. A solitary existence could be lonely, but it was also safer. That's how Hugh saw it.

He looked toward the house, wondering again about the woman inside. Living here alone couldn't be easy. Surely she could find another husband without much effort, as pretty as she was. But there was something else about her, something that made him think of a canary in a cage.

There are many kinds of prisons. That thought was followed with words he'd read in the Bible that morning. *Stand fast therefore in the liberty wherewith Christ hath made us free, and be not entangled again with the yoke of bondage.*

Hugh had a talent for memorizing, an aptitude he'd honed over the years. Too often he hadn't had easy access to books so he'd learned to commit words to memory. That way, he always had a story to remember. That talent was proving a blessing as he sought to have a better understanding of his Savior.

His mother had had a strong faith in God. Hugh remembered that about her. He'd always known it. Why had it taken him so many years to come to believe for himself? Maybe his father had something to do with it. Sweeney Brennan hadn't believed in much beyond the next bottle.

God, help me learn to forgive him.

It wasn't the first time he'd prayed those words. Probably wouldn't be the last. Not until he got an answer. Not until he was able to let go of the memories. Not until the pain of betrayal lost its grip upon his heart.

Four

"Please be careful, Mr. Brennan." Julia shaded her eyes against the glare of the sun.

She'd noticed the hole in the barn roof earlier this spring, but there had always seemed to be something more important to do—with her time as well as her money—than repair it. The weather had been fine for weeks. It could wait to be patched, she'd reasoned.

Hugh Brennan thought otherwise—which was why he was up on the roof now, doing a balancing act on the ridgeline.

A fall will kill him.

Hugh wasn't the sort of man who let the grass grow under his feet, that was for certain. In the past twenty-four hours, he'd mended the fence in the paddock behind the barn, organized the tools above the workbench, and given his living quarters a thorough cleaning. And now he planned to patch that hole in the barn roof—if he didn't kill himself first.

She released a held breath when he reached his destination and knelt down. In that position, he seemed more secure. Perhaps that was an illusion, but she took comfort in it anyway.

How strange. Why should she take comfort in his safety? Why should she *need* comfort? He wasn't a friend or even a true ranch hand. He was a drifter, a stranger from Illinois on his way to Idaho. No one of importance in her life. Not really. She supposed the comfort was because, as a Christian, she should care about her fellow man. *Any* fellow man.

But that doesn't mean I need to stand here gawking at him, as if I have no work of my own to do.

And yet she had no desire to look away. The truth was, it wasn't only concern for his safety that kept her eyes on him. There was something pleasing about watching him work. Perhaps it was his dark good looks. No, she'd learned that physical appearance alone did not draw her interest. There was something else about Hugh. She wished she could put her finger on it.

Drawing a deep breath, she turned away from the barn and moved with resolution toward the house. Today she meant to tackle the laundry, her least favorite chore, and one she too often put off until later.

"Rejoice in all things," she whispered. "I'm not doing very well at that, am I, God?" The question made her shake her head. She would need to change a great deal before she successfully practiced that biblical command. "The spirit indeed is willing, but the flesh is weak."

Inside, Julia set to work, scrubbing the clothes and linens that had soaked overnight. The task took a good couple of hours, but it seemed like much longer and left her arms sore and her back aching. Next she rinsed the laundry—first in plain water, then in bluing—and then everything went into a large basket that she carried outside so she could hang the clean clothes and linens on the line.

It was there Hugh joined her.

"The roof's fixed," he said. "Let me help you with this." He pulled a sheet from the basket and shook it, being careful to keep it from touching the ground.

Julia knew she was staring at him as if he'd sprouted another head, but she couldn't seem to stop herself.

A wry smile curved the corners of his mouth. "Doesn't hurt a man to help with the laundry. Not if he appreciates clean clothes and bedding." He dropped the sheet over the line. "And I do appreciate such things. More than you know."

In all her years of marriage, no one had ever

helped Julia with the laundry. Not even when she was big with—

She clamped down on the thought, not allowing it to fully form. Remembering was too painful.

"Something wrong, ma'am?"

She looked at Hugh; his brown eyes were filled with concern. "No," she answered at last. "Nothing." She grabbed one of her skirts from the basket and took it to an empty space on the clothesline.

"If I said something to upset you—"

"You didn't." She drew a deep breath and faced him again. "Truly you didn't. I'm just so used to spending my days alone, I'm not very good at carrying on a conversation."

His jaw clenched and released. "I'm a lot like that, Mrs. Grace. I've spent a good share of my life alone with my own thoughts."

"Call me Julia."

"Julia."

"You never married?" she asked him.

"No." He shook his head, then retrieved another item to hang on the line. "Never had much opportunity."

A good-looking man like you? She was grateful the words stayed in her mind rather than escaping her mouth. Especially since she knew good looks did not make a man good. He could be attractive and also be cruel or unkind or

40

thoughtless. She'd learned that lesson well. And to be honest, it bothered her that she even noticed Hugh's physical appearance. It wasn't like her. Hadn't been like her for years.

"If you don't mind me asking, Julia, how long have you been widowed?"

Perhaps she should mind, but she didn't. Perhaps she shouldn't answer, but she did. "A year and a bit."

"Not long then. I reckon it's hard to talk about still."

"Yes." *But not for the reasons you think.*

It puzzled Hugh, this desire to know more about Julia Grace. Even more surprising was his seeming willingness to respond to whatever she said or asked. He hadn't spoken as many words to any single individual in the past decade. At least not in a few days' time.

"I'm sorry for your loss," he added softly. He knew something about loss, and whatever pain she felt, he wished he could ease it for her.

"Thank you." She seemed ready to say more, but Bandit hopped up from where he'd been lying in the shade and went to stand beside his mistress, hackles raised. Julia looked toward the barnyard as two men rode into view. She drew a deep breath before saying, "It's okay, Bandit. It's just Charlie." Then she walked out to meet them in the barnyard.

Hugh stayed where he was, half-hidden by a sheet on the line.

"Afternoon, Julia," one of the men said.

"Charlie. What brings you to Sage-hen?"

"We came by to tell you I lost a couple of cows to a wolf attack earlier in the week. Thought you should know so you can be on the lookout."

"Thanks. I appreciate it."

"I've got some of my men out hunting for the wolf now."

"Just one?"

"That's what the tracks suggest." The man named Charlie motioned with his head toward Bandit. "You might want to make sure that dog of yours stays close to home. He's too old to outrun a wolf."

"Bandit doesn't ever get too far from me. We take care of each other."

Charlie leaned a forearm on the saddle horn. "Wish you'd sell me this place, Julia. Then you wouldn't have to depend on a dog to take care of you."

Hugh saw Julia's back stiffen and wondered what expression she wore.

"I appreciate your concern." Her tone said otherwise.

"You shouldn't be on this place alone."

There was a lengthy pause before she answered, "I'm not alone." She glanced over her shoulder toward Hugh. "I've hired a man to help around the place."

Something in her eyes—hard to say what exactly —caused Hugh to step out from behind the sheet. After a moment, she faced Charlie again, and Hugh turned his gaze in the same direction.

He knew the look of a dangerous man when he saw one . . . and he saw one now.

For years, Julia had tried not to dislike Charlie Prescott. After all, the only thing she truly had against her brother-in-law was his blood relationship to Angus.

Yes, Charlie had hired on the men who used to work for her husband. But how could she object when she hadn't had the money to keep them working for her? She should be glad that they'd found employment without having to look far and wide. She *was* glad for them.

Yes, it irritated her that Charlie persisted in trying to buy Sage-hen from her. She wished he would accept her decision to stay and work the ranch herself. But that was no reason to dislike him either.

No, Charlie had not wronged her. Not really. His biggest flaw was that he looked and sounded too much like Angus Grace. At least that's what she told herself as she glanced at him and tried to subdue a tiny shiver that moved up her spine.

"Who is he?" Charlie asked.

"His name is Brennan. Hugh Brennan."

"He's not from around here."

"No, he isn't."

"I don't like it, Julia."

I don't care what you like.

"How long's he been working for you?"

"Not long." *Not that it's any of your business.*

Charlie shook his head. "Angus always said you were a hard one to keep in line."

It was as if she could feel the back of a hand connect with her jaw. Although she knew no one had touched her, she felt herself fly backward and slam against a wall. Fear and pain exploded inside of her. So real. So familiar. She wanted to run and hide. She wanted to curl into a ball and pray for protection. But somehow she did neither. She stood her ground and met Charlie's too-much-like-Angus's blue eyes with what she hoped was a confident expression.

"Did he?" She shrugged. "I didn't know that." The latter was a falsehood. Angus had said it to her face more than once.

Charlie straightened in the saddle. "Well, keep an eye out for that wolf. Don't want you losing any of your herd. You can't afford it."

She nodded, though what she wanted was to tell him he was wrong. Only he wasn't. She couldn't afford to lose any of her cattle. Not to wolves or weather or any other cause.

With one last glance toward Hugh, Charlie turned his horse and rode away, his ranch hand quickly doing the same. Julia stayed where she was until they were out of sight.

"Who was that?"

She released a soft gasp of surprise. She hadn't heard Hugh's approach, hadn't known he now stood so close behind her. "My brother-in-law." She turned to face him. "His name is Charlie Prescott. He owns a neighboring spread to the north of here."

"Are you all right?"

"All right?"

"Did he threaten you?" A shadow covered his face. "You seem upset."

Julia looked up to see if the day had turned cloudy, but the sky was clear.

"If there's something you need—"

"I don't need anything."

"If you're sure."

Odd, wasn't it? That Charlie, who she'd known for more than a decade, made her feel so uneasy, though without reason. But that Hugh, who she'd known a matter of days, made her feel safe, protected. Also without reason? "I'm fine, Hugh. Thanks."

He continued to watch her, but she had no idea what he thought. His expression gave away no clues.

"I'd best finish hanging the laundry," she said.

"Maybe you should take care of feeding the livestock." She sounded abrupt although she hadn't meant to.

He tugged on the brim of his hat. "Yes, ma'am. I'll get right to it." He turned on his heel.

"Hugh."

He stopped and looked back.

"I meant it. Thank you. For all you've done around the place while you've been here."

He gave her one of those lopsided half-smiles before nodding and heading toward the barn once again.

Rose Collins was on the way to the barn when she saw Charlie Prescott and another cowboy cantering their horses down the road. There was only one reason for him to be out this way—he'd called on Julia again.

Wretched man.

Fear niggled at her spine. What would happen if Charlie Prescott got his hands on Sage-hen? He would turn his attention to her family's farm, that's what. He was the type of man who would never have enough. He was hungry for more and more land, more and more cattle, more and more wealth, more and more power. Julia didn't think Charlie was cruel like Angus had been. Rose thought he might be worse, in a different way.

She stepped into the shadowy interior of the barn and stopped to allow her eyes to adjust. Then she made her way to the stall where Peter was doctoring an injured colt.

"I just saw Mr. Prescott coming down the road from Julia's place," she said.

Her husband glanced up. "She won't sell to him."

"She might not have a choice. She's got nobody to help her. Prescott hired away the men who used to work for Angus. Who's she gonna get to help her drive the cattle to the Double T?"

"Guess if needs be, I could go with her."

"You've got a good heart, Peter Collins, and I love you all the more for wanting to help your neighbor every way you can. But you know good and well you've already got all you can do here on your own place."

He set down the colt's leg. "Rosie girl, I guess we'll have to trust the Lord to provide."

God knew she loved her husband. Had loved him since she first laid eyes on him when she was a girl of fourteen. But sometimes his easygoing nature made her feel like shaking him until his teeth rattled. Sure, she knew she was supposed to trust the Lord and not worry about tomorrow. Easier said than done, especially when they had ten children to feed and clothe. Ten daughters, Abigail the oldest at seventeen and Jemima the youngest at two months. Every last one of them loved and wanted, no doubt about it. Still, it wasn't easy providing for a large family.

"Rosie—" Peter stepped out of the stall— "we've done fine all these years. We'll do fine in the years to come. You'll see."

She shook her head. "Angus Grace was a mean sort. You know how I felt about him and the way he treated Julia. Can't help thinking the world's a better place without him in it, God have mercy on his miserable soul. But I don't trust Charlie Prescott. He might seem nicer on the outside, but I don't think he is. He wants Sagehen, and if he gets it, he'll want our land next. Nothing he has will ever be enough. Mark my words."

"Let's let tomorrow's trouble take care of itself." Peter put his arm around her shoulders and leaned close to plant a kiss on the top of her head.

Rose sighed. Her husband would never change, and she was glad of it. He kept her on a steady course, this man of the soil. They'd had twenty years as husband and wife and had come through plenty of life's storms. But they'd seen them through side-by-side.

Giving her shoulder a squeeze, Peter said, "If God is for us, who can be against us?"

No, nothing she said would change her husband, and she wouldn't want it to. So she simply smiled up at him before leaning her head against his shoulder as they walked out of the barn together.

Five

Hugh awakened on Sunday morning to the sound of rain on the barn and thunder rolling in the distance. Satisfaction with a job well-done brought a smile to his lips. He'd patched the roof just in time. The loft would stay dry no matter how long or hard it stormed.

Lying on his back, he put his hands under his head and stared at the ceiling. The cool air that swirled through the open door smelled fresh and moist. And despite the room being almost as small as a prison cell, no dread of a closed space threatened. Not this morning. He'd slept sound, without any nightmares. Maybe the bad memories were beginning to fade. Maybe, with God's help, they wouldn't torture him any longer.

Closing his eyes, he thanked the Lord for His tender mercies, then pushed off the covers and sat up. Another clap of thunder sounded, this one much closer than the last. His horse—in one of the stalls to protect his bad leg—snorted his objection to the clatter.

At supper the previous evening, Julia had informed Hugh that he wasn't expected to do any work on the Lord's Day other than to make certain the livestock had food and water. He'd asked if she would be going into town to attend church services in the morning, thinking he might join her. She'd answered with a shake of her head but had given no reason. He wondered why. What could the reason be? He was certain she was a believer.

But it's not my business why.

He rose, poured some water into a large porcelain bowl, and washed his face. After dressing, he left his quarters, walking to the barn door. He didn't have to open it to know it was raining cats and dogs. He opened it anyway.

The heavens were a dark pewter, slung low to the earth, the barnyard all puddles and mud. No chickens were visible outside the coop. Smart birds. A horse in the nearby corral stood with his rump to the wind, his head down and eyes closed. A glance toward the house told Hugh his employer hadn't slept in. Smoke was momentarily visible above the cook-stove chimney before being swept away by the storm.

The front door opened, and Julia stepped onto the porch just as a flash of lightning illuminated the barnyard, followed a heartbeat later by a crash of thunder. The entire barn seemed to shudder, and Hugh flinched, half-expecting the building to tumble down around his ears.

Mighty glad I'm not out in this, Lord. Thanks for providing a place to stay.

"Mr. Brennan!"

He looked toward the porch again and saw Julia motion for him to join her.

"Breakfast," she added before returning inside.

There was no way to get to the house without getting soaked, but he wasn't about to forego a meal because of rain. He leaned the top of his head into the wind and ran across the barnyard, trying to avoid the deeper puddles the best he could. In a matter of seconds, he was on the porch—and dripping from head to foot. He stepped to the threshold but stopped there and looked inside.

"Come in, Mr. Brennan," Julia said as she attended to something on the stove.

"I . . . uh . . . I'll drip all over your floors. And my boots are muddy."

She glanced toward the door, a look of surprise in her eyes. Then she released a wry laugh—or so it seemed to Hugh. "You won't track in anything the floors haven't seen before. But I'll get you a towel so you can dry off a bit. No point you catching cold from the damp."

"Thanks, ma'am."

She cocked an eyebrow at him.

"Julia," he corrected.

After she left the kitchen, Hugh leaned against the doorjamb and removed his boots, stepping into the parlor in his stocking feet. The right sock had a hole over his big toe. He thought to tug at the sock to try to hide its pitiful state, but Julia returned before he could.

As she handed him the towel, she said, "That sock could use mending before you get a blister from your boot."

" 'Fraid I don't have a needle." He shrugged, embarrassed. Ashamed to admit he hadn't had the money to replace something so inexpensive. "Lost it along the trail."

But it wasn't judgment he saw in her eyes. It was compassion. "I have needles and lots of thread. If you'll bring me what needs mending, I'll see to it."

"I couldn't ask you to do my sewing for me. But I'd borrow that needle and use some of your thread."

There was that flicker of surprise in her eyes again. And just as quick as the last time, it disappeared, only this time she didn't laugh or smile. "As you wish." She turned from him. "Now you'd better sit down and eat. Your breakfast is getting cold."

A restless energy swirled inside of Julia as she ate her breakfast. She kept her eyes averted from the man on the opposite side of the table. Hugh's mere presence seemed to make her say and do foolish things. Darn his socks! Why ever would she volunteer to do such a thing? Of course she would let him borrow a needle. In fact, she would give him one—and some thread to go with it—but it wasn't her place to take on his mending. She was his employer, not his wife.

Wife? The word caused a shudder to run through her, turning the food in her stomach to stone. Her appetite lost, she set down her fork and turned her gaze toward the nearest window. The rain still fell in torrents beyond the glass.

"Good thing you weren't planning a trip into town for church," Hugh said.

"Indeed."

"Do you usually attend services?"

She shook her head. "No." She pressed her lips together, trying to bite back the remainder of her response, but the desire for honesty won over the desire for discretion. "My husband wasn't a believer . . . and he didn't approve of me making that long ride into Pine Creek without him. So I learned to keep the Lord's Day in my own way here on the ranch."

"That's how it's been for me."

She looked at him.

"You know. Traveling west, being on the trail, not staying in towns most of the time. I see in the Bible that we're to gather with other believers, but that's not always possible, is it?"

"No," she said softly, "it isn't."

"Do you think we might have church together, you and me, here in the kitchen?" He leaned forward on his chair, an expression of eagerness in his eyes. " 'Where two or more are gathered.' Isn't that what it says?"

It was ridiculous, the way her heart leapt at Hugh's suggestion. She was used to worshiping God alone. She *liked* worshiping Him alone. It was a sacred time, not meant to be shared with a stranger.

Only . . . Hugh Brennan didn't seem a stranger. She'd known him just a few days, but something about him—something in his dark brown eyes, his voice, his manner—made it feel as if they'd known each other much longer. Strangely, she was comfortable in his company, and that very comfortableness made her uncomfortable. She didn't like feeling that way about him. It could be a mistake. A big mistake.

And yet—

"It would mean a lot to me," he added softly.

"All right. After I've washed the breakfast dishes."

He grinned. "I can wash them if you'd like."

Hanging laundry? Avoiding tracking mud into house? Mending socks? Washing dishes? Hugh Brennan was unlike any man she'd ever known. "Thank you, but I'll do them."

"How about you wash and I'll dry? It'll go faster."

To continue to refuse would be rude, she decided, and so she gave him a nod.

...

By the time Hugh and Julia sat down at the kitchen table a second time—the dishes washed, dried, and put away—the thunder and lightning had moved to the other side of the mountain range to the east. It still rained, but the storm was gentler now, the droplets playing a softer melody as they spattered the rooftop and windows.

Hugh was the one who'd suggested this worship service for two, but he hadn't expected to feel such a sense of holiness as he listened to Julia read aloud from her Bible. Light from the lamp she'd placed in the center of the table cast a warm glow upon her face and hair.

Entertaining angels unaware. Where had he heard that expression? He wasn't sure, but it seemed to describe her. She was like an angel, giving him shelter and work, treating him with kindness and goodness, despite the caution he saw in her eyes every now and then.

Julia stopped reading and glanced up. "Would you like to read for a spell?"

"Mind if I just listen? The words sound better coming from you."

"I doubt that." She tilted her head slightly to one side, giving it a slight shake. "I've never known another man, outside of a couple of pastors maybe, who'd want to sit down and listen to me read the Bible aloud. This is . . . nice."

Although she smiled slightly at the end, Hugh

suspected there was pain hidden in her words. A sorrow that went deep and was intensely private. He found himself wishing he knew the cause so that he could then attempt to wipe it away. Foolish, he supposed, knowing the secret pain in his own heart that he expected would be with him forever.

Six

Come Monday morning, there wasn't a cloud left in the sky, although the proof of the previous day's storm was evident in the lingering puddles in the barnyard.

Shortly after breakfast—when Julia had informed Hugh the two of them would be going into Pine Creek to get supplies—they led the two work horses out of the paddock and harnessed them to the wagon. Bandit circled the vehicle, people, and horses several times, almost as if making sure they completed the task correctly. Satisfied, the spaniel jumped into the wagon bed.

Julia laughed. "How often are you left behind, fella?"

Bandit wagged his tale.

With a boot on the wheel hub, Julia stepped up to the wagon seat and took the reins in hand. Hugh joined her a moment later. She slapped the reins against the horses' rumps, and the wagon jerked into motion. They rode in comfortable silence; the horses followed a winding trail for a mile or so before they came to the main road. Then she turned the team north. Tree-covered mountains rose in the distance ahead of them and on both east and west sides.

"That's my nearest neighbor's place," Julia said, pointing toward a house and barn a short distance back from the road. "The Collins' family. They've got ten children. All girls."

"Ten daughters?"

"Yes. The oldest is seventeen. Youngest is a couple of months old. Jemima Ruth is the baby's name." A mixture of joy and sorrow filled her chest. "I helped deliver little Jem."

Even as the words came out of Julia's mouth, she wished she could take them back. They revealed too much. They told this man, this stranger seated beside her, that she longed for a baby of her own. Did he wonder why she was childless after eleven years of marriage? No. How could he? She hadn't told him how long she'd been married to Angus. For all Hugh Brennan knew, they'd been married no time at all. Not even long enough for her to become pregnant.

Which, of course, was not true.

Tears stung her eyes, and her throat constricted. Perhaps if she hadn't—

She cut off the thought before it could completely materialize. The past was the past.

She couldn't change it. She couldn't wish it away. Angus was gone, and she was childless. That was how she would remain. She would live alone on Sage-hen for the rest of her life. She would grow old alone and die alone.

"What's the name of the town where we're headed?" Hugh asked, intruding on her thoughts. "You told me but I forgot."

Bless him. He'd seen her distress and taken pity. "Pine Creek," she answered—and was thankful that her voice sounded normal.

"I'd started to believe Wyoming was mostly sagebrush, jackrabbits, and antelope. But those mountains . . ." He let his words drift off, then gave an expressive whistle.

"The Rocky Mountains," she said. "They go all the way up into Canada and all the way down to New Mexico. I read somewhere that the range is about three thousand miles long. Magnificent, aren't they?"

"Nothing like them between here and Illinois, that's for sure. There's hills and valleys, but nothing like the Rockies. A lot of the land's flatter than a pancake where I hail from."

"I've lived in or near the mountains my whole life. Don't think I'd care to stay where I couldn't see them."

"Always lived in Wyoming?"

She slapped the reins, encouraging a faster walk from the horses. "No. I was born in Idaho.

Up in Grand Coeur. It's an old gold town, although by the time I came along, the rush was pretty much over. Still lots of mining and miners, but not quite as lawless as the camps were in the beginning." She wouldn't bother to tell him that her mother had worked in one of the saloons—and still did, as far as she knew—or that she had never known her father. She wasn't sure her mother knew who he was. If Angus Grace hadn't come along when Julia was seventeen, she might have found herself forced to work in a saloon too.

Would that life have been worse than marriage to Angus?

Perhaps. Perhaps not. But she supposed that's why the Lord told her she had to trust Him. Because only He had answers to the "what ifs" in life.

Rejoice evermore, the Bible said. She had a long way to go in that regard. She hadn't yet learned to rejoice in every circumstance. She tried, and she was better now than she used to be. But then, Angus was dead, so maybe it was simply easier now.

Peter Collins leaned his forearms on the top rail of the corral fence. A frown creased his brow as he stared toward the road. Julia Grace had passed by in her wagon a short while before—a man beside her on the seat—and seeing her had brought back his wife's concerns about Charlie

Prescott. Sure, Peter had told Rose she didn't have to worry. That didn't stop him from doing some worrying of his own.

If Charlie Prescott was ever able to get his hands on the Grace property—through scrupulous or unscrupulous means—Peter feared he might cut off the water supply to this farm so fast it would make Peter's head spin. Charlie wouldn't have to offer to buy the land again. He'd be able to wait for the Collins family to go broke.

He gave his head a firm shake and practiced taking every thought captive, especially those bad ones.

Peter never failed to acknowledge that the good Lord had blessed him in more ways than he could count. But he could count some of them: He was married to a woman he loved to distraction and who loved him in return. His children were healthy, good-natured, and for the most part, obedient. They weren't a wealthy family and never would be, but they had everything they needed and a few things they wanted. He and Rose both believed in and trusted the Almighty and were raising their children to do the same. And there was the beauty of God's world to be seen whenever they stepped outside their front door.

He gave his head another slow shake as he pushed off the fence. No, he couldn't count all the ways God had blessed him. Weren't enough hours in the day. So he might as well go inside the house and kiss a few of those blessings—his wife and new baby daughter included.

What was it about Julia Grace that made Hugh want to leap to her defense? No one else was around, and yet he had the desire to protect and shelter her. Was it the delicacy of her appearance, a fragile beauty unlike any he remembered seeing before? That she should be seated next to a man like him seemed all wrong.

Silence stretched between them again, the only sound the clopping of hooves, the creak of the wagon, and the jangle of harness. While Hugh had plenty more questions he could have asked his employer, he chose to refrain. Because the more questions he asked of her, the more permission he gave for her to ask questions of her own. Questions he might not want to answer. Answers that might make her tell him to leave, and he didn't want to leave. Not yet.

He turned to look toward the rugged mountains rising on his right, a mass of granite covered in wild flowers and pine trees. A landscape of gray and purple and green. It seemed to him that God had done some of His best work in western Wyoming.

Which by his strength setteth fast the mountains.

How had God decided where to put mountains and where to put oceans and where to put deserts? Had the Father, Son, and Holy Ghost debated such matters before the world was spoken into existence or had the Trinity been in complete agreement from the beginning of time?

He gave his head a slow shake. Were such thoughts proper? He hoped the Lord was amused rather than angered by them. Sometimes in the night, when he was unable to sleep, he liked to imagine himself walking beside Jesus near the Sea of Galilee. Hugh could envision the Lord laughing when he posed such questions to Him, but He would answer. He wouldn't think Hugh stupid for not knowing.

There was comfort in that belief.

Bandit began barking, drawing Hugh's attention to the wagon bed. The spaniel had his front legs up on the sideboards.

"No, Bandit," Julia said. "Stay."

The dog stopped barking, but his body twitched with excitement.

"No, Bandit."

Hugh tried to follow the line of the dog's gaze but saw nothing amiss.

"A wolf," Julia said, as if reading his thoughts.

"Where?"

"There." She pointed. "Near that dead tree. He's running toward the base of the mountain. Probably the one Charlie warned me about."

It took Hugh awhile, but he found the gray shadow before it disappeared into a draw.

"This past winter was milder than most. I

didn't have any trouble with wolves. Guess they had plenty of easy pickings among the deer and elk up higher in the mountains. It isn't always like that. When the snows get really deep and hunting is scarce, the wolves and other predators can ruin a herd."

Hugh pictured Julia taking aim and firing—and imagined her flying backward, knocked off her feet by the kick of the weapon. She was gutsy. He'd say that for her.

"I'd rather have to run off the wolves than a grizzly."

"Grizzly?" He turned toward her again.

"Grizzly bears. Cantankerous, enormous creatures. Sometimes they kill for sport more than food. Least, that's what Angus used to say. They tend to stay further north of here, up in the Yellowstone, but there've been a couple who've come down this far since I've been at Sage-hen." She gave a slight shudder. "I saw one from a distance once. I'll never forget it. Gives me nightmares."

"I get the feeling not much scares you, Julia."

"Plenty of things scare me. I just try not to let my fears get the upper hand."

" 'For God hath not given us the spirit of fear; but of power, and of love, and of a sound mind.' "

"Second Timothy 1:7. You know your Scriptures."

"I'm doing my best to know them." He shrugged.

"Traveling alone, a man's got time to do plenty of reading."

A puzzled frown furrowed her brow. "I'm not quite sure what to make of you, Hugh." Her gaze returned to the road ahead, and she slapped the reins. "Get up there, boys." After a moment's silence, she added, "We'll be to Pine Creek in another hour."

Seven

Julia supposed Pine Creek was like a thousand other small towns west of the Mississippi. It had its Main Street and its First Street. It had a doctor and pharmacy, two churches, a general mercantile, a feed store, and a sheriff's office and jail. It had its one-room schoolhouse, the pride of the town council. It had its lawyer and its blacksmith and its livery and its saloons; two of the latter—plenty enough for a town of its size. Two too many, Julia would have said. She'd never seen anything but heartache come out of drinking establishments.

As the wagon pulled past Lucky Luke's and the tinkle of piano keys spilled from the saloon, she felt a sting in her chest, a sudden longing for her mother. It still hurt, five years after she'd written her mother a letter filled with hateful words. She'd tried to apologize, of course. She'd written a number of letters after that one, asking for her mother's forgiveness. But Madeline Crane had returned Julia's letters unopened, and finally Julia had ceased to write. She supposed she couldn't blame her mother. If only—

If only . . . if only . . . if only . . . Thinking those horrid little words changed nothing. She couldn't undo the past. She couldn't go back and refuse to marry Angus and stay in Grand Coeur. She couldn't bring her babies back from heaven. She couldn't—

She pushed away the memories as the wagon arrived at the mercantile. "We'll pick up supplies here first, then go to the feed store," she said to Hugh, wrapping the reins around the brake handle.

"All right." He hopped to the ground.

She did the same from her side of the wagon. "Bandit, you wait here." The spaniel lay down, head on paws, giving her a doleful look, and Julia reached over the side of the bed to give him a pat on the head. "I know, but I won't be long."

Hugh observed her and Bandit from the boardwalk, the hint of a smile once more in the corners of his mouth. Something pleasurable curled in her belly. An unexpected sensation. One she didn't welcome.

Flipping strands of hair behind her shoulder with one hand, she moved toward him, studiously avoiding his gaze. "Come along, Mr. Brennan." She stepped onto the boardwalk and lowered her voice. "I reckon it would be better not to use our given names when we're in town."

He gave a brief nod as she walked by him.

The mercantile was a large, rectangular room filled with merchandise on shelves and tables. As always, it seemed to Julia that almost any possible thing a person might want could be found in this store, and what things couldn't be found could be ordered. Not that her needs were great. A good thing since neither were her funds great. She walked to the counter where Nancy Humphrey, the proprietress, stood.

"Mrs. Grace," the woman said, a genuine smile brightening her face. "How good to see you. It's been a long spell since you were last in town."

"Yes, it has."

"Everything all right at your place?"

Julia nodded.

Nancy's gaze shifted beyond Julia's right shoulder.

She didn't have to look to know that Hugh stood not far behind her. "Mrs. Humphrey, this is my hired hand, Mr. Brennan."

"A pleasure to meet you, Mr. Brennan." Nancy nodded in his direction.

Julia pulled the slip of paper from the pocket of her skirt. On it she'd listed the items she most needed to see her through the next month or so. Flour. Salt. Sugar. Coffee. Cornmeal. Vinegar. Oatmeal. Tea. Dried beans. And plenty more. The list was as long as the larder at Sage-hen was close to bare.

"I trust I can put some of this on my account, like I did last year. I'll be selling off some of my herd in a few weeks and can pay the rest of the bill then."

"Of course it's all right. Your husband never failed to pay his bills. Not even in lean years. Mr. Humphrey and I know you'll do the same."

Julia felt herself wince and hoped Nancy didn't notice. But she hated being tied to Angus even after his death. So what if her husband had paid his bills on time and in full? It had nothing to do with her. She was her own woman now. She belonged to no one. She would rise or fall by her own decisions, and God willing, she would make the right ones.

Was Julia as upset as Hugh perceived her to be? He couldn't see her face, her back still to him, and yet there was something about the set of her shoulders that said she was distressed or angry or something.

None of my concern. He needed to remember that. He needed to remember that this was a temporary job for a woman who was nothing more to him than his employer. He was lucky to have the work. Time he settled for being content with that. Time to nip this . . . wanting . . . in the bud.

He turned and moved down one of the narrow

aisles. Without money in his pocket, he wouldn't be buying. And Mrs. Humphrey wasn't likely to extend an unknown ranch hand credit the way she'd extended it to Julia. But it didn't hurt to look around. When he arrived at a display of poles, rods, lines, and other fishing equipment, he stopped.

A memory from long ago returned. A pleasant memory of him and his dad, fishing together. He could hear their laughter mingling on a soft spring breeze. How old would he have been? Maybe fifteen. Sixteen at the oldest. They'd gone to the river early in the morning when the air was cool and fresh. Not only had his dad been sober, but he'd been in one of his rare good moods as well. On that morning, in that moment, Hugh had been glad his dad found him with that family in Nebraska and brought him back to Chicago. He hadn't been glad very often. Only a few years later—

He closed off the thought as he continued down the aisle. There were some things best not remembered. But the memories continued to press in. To escape them, he went outside and stood on the boardwalk, letting his gaze roam over the main street.

Pine Creek wasn't a big place, but it appeared to have all of the necessary businesses to make a town civilized. Not that he was likely to see much of it, it being so far north of the Grace ranch. And once his work for the widow was done, he would leave the area. He'd forget Pine Creek the way he'd forgotten plenty of other small towns between Chicago and this spot on the western edge of Wyoming.

Across the street and down a bit, a man stumbled out of the door of the saloon they'd passed on their way into town. Seeing the drunkard, Hugh was assailed with more memories. Some of the unpleasant ones he tried to avoid. How many times in his young life had he gone looking for his father, usually finding him drunk in a similar establishment? How many times had his father leaned down on Hugh's boyish shoulders and the pair of them stumbled along the streets and back alleys toward whatever place they were able to call home at the time? Even years later, the stench of alcohol, sweat, and vomit seemed to fill his nostrils.

"Mr. Brennan? . . . Hugh?"

Jerked to the present, he turned to find Julia in the doorway of the mercantile, watching him with a puzzled expression.

"Mind helping me load the supplies into the wagon?"

"Sure thing." He would be glad for something to do. Anything to turn his thoughts in a better direction.

A wounded soul could recognize another wounded soul. That was something Julia had learned over the years. She'd seen something in Hugh's eyes a split second before he was able to hide it from her. A look that said he'd known deep betrayal, intense cruelty, or unmentionable sorrow. Perhaps all three. Like Julia.

Suddenly, Hugh was more than a stranger she'd hired to help drive the cattle to market. And perhaps he was also more than she wanted him—or anyone—to be. Because if she could see into him, then he might be able to see into her as well. That would never do.

The two of them loaded the supplies into the wagon in silence, studiously avoiding eye contact. They continued in a similar manner at the feed store, and it wasn't long before the team of horses was pulling the wagon south, Pine Creek growing smaller and smaller behind them.

They might have made it all the way to Sage-hen without exchanging a word if they hadn't met up with Reverend Thomas Peabody, pastor of the Pine Creek Presbyterian Church. Although Julia had seldom attended religious services in town, she liked and respected Reverend Peabody and was glad when he came calling, rare though those visits were.

"Julia Grace," the reverend said, his entire face seeming to crinkle with his smile, "how good to see you."

"And you, Reverend Peabody."

"It's been too long." His kindly gaze shifted to Hugh.

Julia said, "This is Hugh Brennan. He's working for me at the ranch."

"Mr. Brennan. A pleasure."

"Likewise, sir." Hugh bent the brim of his hat as he spoke his greeting.

Turning to Julia again, Reverend Peabody said, "I hope you didn't find the winter too difficult. I heard from Rose Collins that you've had no help on the ranch since last fall. Glad to see that's no longer true. You're well, I trust."

"Yes, I'm well. Thanks."

In the past she'd wondered if this godly man had guessed what sort of husband Angus was. A couple of times, she'd nearly told him, nearly begged him to help her escape. But where would she have gone if she'd left Angus? How would she have made her way? She wasn't schooled beyond the ability to read and write. She had no special skills that would make her desirable as a teacher or a cook or seamstress, no breeding that would make her a suitable companion or governess. What if the only work she could find was in a saloon, entertaining men, like her mother before her? The last question caused her heart to squeeze.

"It was a mild winter," she said. "The cattle weathered it well. They should bring a good price." *Oh, please, God. Let it be so. Let them bring a good price.*

"I assume Mr. Prescott still wants to buy you out."

"That he does, but I have no intention of selling."

"Glad to hear it. Your friends would miss you."

Her chest warmed. "Thank you, Reverend."

"Once again, a pleasure to meet you, Mr. Brennan. I hope I'll have the opportunity to see you again soon."

Hugh nodded.

Reverend Peabody and Julia slapped their reins at the same moment, and the wagon and the buggy moved away in opposite directions.

"Common knowledge, I guess," Hugh said.

"Pardon?"

"About your brother-in-law wanting to buy your place."

"Yes." She glanced at him.

"Is he offering a fair price?"

She thought on that a moment before answering, "Some would say so."

"Maybe you'd be better off selling. You might find life easier elsewhere."

"And go where?" Did his question anger her or frighten her? She wasn't sure, but her tone of voice indicated the former.

"Anywhere you wanted. Another town. Another city. Another country."

"This is my home. I have no intention of leaving just because my life might be easier elsewhere." *I'm safe here. No one can hurt me here.*

"Sorry, Julia. Didn't mean to offend."

She drew a long, deep breath. She shouldn't be so thin-skinned. It was one of her worst flaws. How could this man, this stranger, hope to understand what tied her to Sage-hen?

"I shouldn't have said anything," Hugh added softly.

"No." She shook her head. "It's all right. You have no way of knowing how I feel or why I feel it." She sighed. "I'm not going to sell to Charlie or anyone else. I'm staying right where I am."

He turned his eyes away from her, staring off toward the mountains. "Guess you're lucky then."

"Lucky?"

"Knowing what you want. Some folks live their whole lives without ever finding what they want or where they belong. Some die still trying to figure it out. You're lucky 'cause you already know."

"Are you still looking?" she asked.

He didn't answer. Perhaps he hadn't heard or perhaps he ignored her. She couldn't be sure which.

With the baby in her arms, Rose stepped onto the porch and drew a deep breath. The air was rich with the smell of fresh-turned earth. In the distance, she saw her husband as he followed the team of horses, the sharp blade of the plow carving another row in the field. Peter must have spied her at the same time, for he raised an arm and waved.

There was something wonderful about being married to a man for so long that the two of them thought alike, could finish the other's sentences, knew when they were looking at each other at a distance.

"Ma?" A small hand tugged at her skirt. "I can't read this word."

Rose looked down at the book Gomer held. "Did you ask Abigail to help you?"

The six-year-old shook her head. "She's busy helpin' Faith, and Bathshua's out back, and Charity says I'm not to bother her when she's writin'."

"All right. You take your book back to the table and read the words you can. I'll be in shortly."

After her daughter obeyed, Rose turned toward the field again. Peter had started down another row, his hands grasping the handles of the plow, the leather reins draped over the back of his neck.

Mercy, how she loved that man. How blessed she felt to be his wife and the mother of his children. Of course, when they married, neither of them had envisioned they would be parents to ten daughters. A large family, yes. But all girls? It would have helped if the Lord had seen fit to give them a few sons to work alongside their father. Not that the girls didn't help. They did. But it wasn't quite the same thing.

Shame gave her conscience a quick sting. Shame for complaining, even in a small way. Shame when the Collins' quiver was full to overflowing, while her dear friend's was so empty.

She remembered the first time she'd laid eyes on Julia Grace. Married less than a month. Pretty and delicate. And sporting a black eye that scoundrel of a husband had given her the day before. Not that Julia had said, "Angus hit me." It would be years later before Julia was that honest with Rose. Perhaps because she took the blame for his cruelty upon herself. Perhaps because she feared what would happen if Angus learned of it.

Rose had been taught by her own ma not to think ill of the dead, but it was difficult to come up with anything good to think or say about Angus Grace apart from his handsome face and the way he'd managed his ranch. It seemed to Rose that Julia deserved some peace and rest after all those years with such a brute, but she feared Charlie Prescott wasn't going to give it to her. Land hungry, he was, and plenty persistent.

"Ma!" Gomer called, reminding Rose of her promise.

"Coming, Gomer. I'm coming."

Eight

Hugh leaned against the fence and watched his gelding graze in the shin-high grass. After a week of rest and numerous rubbings of liniment, no sign of the horse's injury remained. Whenever Hugh was ready to leave Sage-hen, his mount would be ready to carry him.

But he wasn't in any hurry to leave—and that surprised him. More than a little.

Movement in the distance caught his attention. He squinted, shading his eyes with one hand. The cattle that had been grazing near the foothills earlier were now trotting toward the north. Something had disturbed them. From what he'd observed in the short while he'd been here, cows didn't stop eating without a good reason.

He pushed off the fence and strode to the house. The front door was open, but he stopped—as he always did—on the threshold. "Julia?"

"Come in, Hugh."

He stepped inside.

She was seated in a chair close to a window, plying the pale yellow fabric in her lap with a needle and thread. Sunlight created something like a halo above her hair.

"I'm going to saddle one of the horses and check on the cattle."

She looked up, a question in her eyes.

"If your brother-in-law or his men got that wolf they were hunting, he'd let you know, wouldn't he?"

"I believe so. Why?" She set aside her sewing.

"Something seems to've spooked the cattle grazing over near the foothills. Thought I'd better have a look, see what it was."

Julia stood. "I'll go with you."

He wondered if she didn't trust him to shoot a wolf if he saw one. Then again, maybe he'd miss if he tried. He was no expert with firearms, be they rifles or pistols.

"Get the horses ready." She headed for her bedroom. "I'll be right out."

By the time Julia emerged from the house, Hugh was waiting with Teddy and another saddle horse near the corral. With a nod in his direction, she slipped her rifle into the scabbard and swung into the saddle. Hugh mounted quickly, and the two of them rode out of the barnyard, cantering east toward the foothills.

She could have let him go on his own, of course. He was capable enough. Over the past couple of days, she'd familiarized him with the layout of the ranch. They'd ridden the boundaries of her land together. She'd shown him the herd and the fences that kept them from straying onto neighboring land. He'd learned the best place to cross the river that cut through a corner of Sage-hen.

It confounded her how quickly he'd become a part of her daily routine. Even more surprising, she wasn't afraid when she was with him. Like her good friend and neighbor, Peter Collins, she felt an innate trust when she was in Hugh's presence. Unlike Peter, there was no logical reason to trust Hugh. Not really. Not when she knew so little about him. But she did trust him. She could only pray to God that she wasn't proving herself a fool once again.

The rolling landscape obscured the place where Hugh said he'd seen the cattle, and when they topped the final rise, Julia felt relief flow through her. No cow or calf lay in view, a predator feasting on its kill. There was no blood to be seen to indicate an attack of any sort. And most of all, Bandit gave no cry of alarm.

She reined in, and Hugh did likewise.

"They were headed in that direction," Hugh said, pointing toward the north. "Following that line of trees."

She nudged Teddy with her heels, and as the horse moved slowly forward, Julia studied the ground. Years before, a ranch hand had explained to her how to track a wild animal. *"To start with, Miz Grace, you have to know how and where to look,"* he'd told her, *"not just what to look for. The signs are there if you're payin' attention."*

Angus had fired that friendly young cowboy the next day. Julia never did learn to track wild animals. Not really. Good thing she had Bandit.

Looking up, she said, "Let's see where the cows went." She turned Teddy in the direction Hugh had indicated, setting the pace at a gentle lope. Bandit raced ahead of them, happy and looking for small animals to chase. The last of Julia's concern drained away. They could turn around and go back if they wanted. No predator threatened the herd. She was sure of it. But she was content to keep riding, the sun on her face, the breeze tugging at her hair.

"Guess I was wrong," Hugh said after a lengthy silence.

"Better safe than sorry."

"I'm not much of a cowboy."

She gave him a quick smile. "You learn fast."

He looked like he would respond, but before he could, the cows they'd sought came into view. Julia and Hugh reined their horses to a stop. Some of the herd lifted their heads to look at them, then went back to grazing. Several calves cavorted, looking almost as if they were playing a game of tag.

"I love this time of year," Julia said softly.

Hugh must have heard her, for he looked her way, as if waiting for her to expand upon her comment.

In a whisper, she said, "New life. Fresh hope."

And then her thoughts hurtled back to a distant spring when she'd been young—and even a little hopeful.

"Julia, sit still and look at me."

When her mama spoke in that tone of voice, Julia was quick to obey. To do otherwise, she'd learned, would earn her a swat on the bottom and time spent sitting on a small stool in the corner. Julia hated the second even more than the first.

"You're not to leave this house while Mama's at work. Do you understand?"

"I get scared alone," Julia replied. "It's dark and I hear things."

Mama's expression softened. "Oh, my darlin' girl. I know. I know you get scared when it's dark and I'm not here and this old place creaks and groans. But I have to work or we'd go hungry. We wouldn't have this little house, such as it is, to live in if it wasn't for my work at the saloon. One day we'll leave Grand Coeur and go some place far from here. Like a couple of birds, we'll just fly away. Someday you'll live in a nice home and nobody'll look down on you no more. I swear it. If it's the last thing I ever do, I swear I'll make sure you don't have to live the rest of your life the way I've had to live mine. I want you to stretch your wings, my darlin' girl, and learn to soar."

Julia wasn't sure what her mama meant by all she said, but she nodded as if she understood.

"I love you," Mama added, cupping Julia's chin in her hand. "When you get scared in the night, you just pull those covers over your head and you hear me say those words. Okay?"

Again she nodded.

"Someday it'll be better." Mama turned and looked toward the window. "Someday it will."

"New life. Fresh hope."

Julia's simple words, spoken poignantly, had made Hugh think of his youngest sister. He didn't know why. Julia didn't resemble Diana. Unlike Hugh or Felicia, his baby sister had taken after their mother—red hair, green eyes, pale complexion. He recalled her as adorable and impish. Even when she got caught in some mischief, she'd managed to escape punishment. Even their drunk of a father had favored Diana, the child who saw the world through rose-colored glasses. He wondered if she still saw it that way, eighteen years later.

"My goodness," Julia said. "We both grew rather pensive."

He cleared his throat of unwelcome emotion. "Yeah, I guess we did." He looked up the hillside to his right—and for just a moment, thought he saw something among the trees. Maybe a horse and rider? He squinted. No, he didn't see any movement. But the hair on the back of his neck seemed to stand on end, and the feeling unsettled him.

"Shall we go back, Mr. Brennan?"

"If it's all the same to you, I think I'll ride the fence line while I'm out this way." He looked at her again. "I'll be back by suppertime."

She returned his gaze for a moment, then called for Bandit and turned her horse toward the house.

Hugh watched her go and wondered what made her want to remain on this ranch so far from civilization. Alone. Unprotected. Vulnerable. He wished . . .

He shook his head and looked once more toward the trees on the hillside. Nothing there. His eyes were playing tricks on him. So were the hairs on his neck.

He nudged the horse forward. They moved down a slope and rode through the cows and up to the fence that followed the hillside about twenty yards from the copse of trees. There they stopped, and Hugh's eyes once again raked the area. Only when he was completely satisfied did he ride on.

Nine

Another Sunday arrived, but unlike the previous week, this one dawned with clear skies. As soon as her morning chores were done, Julia saddled Teddy and rode to her favorite spot on the river. There, in the shade of several tall pine trees, Bandit exploring nearby, she spread a blanket and opened her Bible.

A few times in the early years of her marriage, she'd railed at God or begged Him to rescue her. More than once she'd demanded to know why things were as they were. There had been periods when she was convinced God thought even less of her than Angus did. Not true, of course. The Lord loved her. Somehow He'd broken through her fear, pain, and anger and revealed Himself and His love. When she couldn't think of anything else to thank Him for, she always thanked Him for that.

This morning, she lay on her back on the huge rock that jutted over a bend in the river and called out a portion of a favorite Psalm:

For there is not a word in my tongue,
  but lo, O LORD, thou knowest it altogether.
Thou hast beset me behind and before,
  and laid thine hand upon me.

She smiled as she let her eyes close. How marvelous to understand that no matter what path she was on, God went before her and He was also behind her. He enclosed her. His hand was upon her. What a difference it made, knowing it. If only she could be conscious of it at all times.

"I'm trying, Father."

Keeping her eyes closed, she sought to be still, she sought to listen to Him. But it wasn't God's quiet voice that came to her. It was Hugh Brennan's: *"Some folks live their whole lives without ever knowing what they want or where they belong."*

His comment left her oddly disturbed. But why should that be so? She *did* belong here. Sage-hen was her home. True, at one time it had seemed more of a prison, but now it was her sanctuary.

"One day we'll leave Grand Coeur and go some place far from here. Like a couple of birds, we'll just fly away . . . I want you to stretch your wings, my darlin' girl, and learn to soar."

Julia opened her eyes and saw the trees above her sway in a gust of wind. A dozen or so birds abandoned their resting places, flying high and fast, as if giving her an example of what her mother had wanted for her so long ago.

If Julia had wings, where would they take her? What would she want to see? A big city? Perhaps San Francisco or New York. Another country? France or Italy or maybe Greece. The ocean? Any ocean. But try as she might, she couldn't imagine herself anywhere but here. Even her childhood in Idaho seemed to have happened to someone else, more dreams than memories.

"Would you still want me to fly away, Mama?" she wondered aloud.

Madeline Crane had always wanted something better, something different for her daughter. She'd done what she could to make sure Julia escaped the kind of life she'd had. But it had all turned out so very wrong, and Julia had blamed her mother for that.

"I'm sorry, Mama. I know God forgives me for the harsh words I wrote to you. I regret them so much. I hope you know I love you. Someday I hope you'll forgive me too. If only I knew where you were. If only . . ."

She rolled onto her stomach. Lifting her upper torso by her forearms, she stared at the flowing water beyond the end of the rock. The river was deep and swift here. And cold. So very, very cold. Several years ago, after miscarrying her last baby, she'd come to this rock and considered throwing herself into the river. In her grief, death had seemed the only answer to her misery. But an unseen hand had fallen upon her shoulder, stopping her. An inaudible voice had spoken comfort into her heart, and somehow she'd found the strength and courage to live on. To face Angus's fury at her continued failure to give him a living child.

Tears sprang to her eyes and slid down her cheeks.

Her babies. She'd wanted her babies. Despite the unhappiness of her marriage and the loathing she'd often felt for her husband, she'd wanted a child. Three times she'd almost had her heart's desire. First there had been a daughter, stillborn at eight months. Then there had been a son, also stillborn. And finally there was the baby she'd lost when only three months gone. She'd nearly died too. The bed had turned crimson with her blood.

Had she lost that baby because Angus hit her? Or had he hit her because she'd lost the baby? It was hard to remember which was cause and which was effect. All she remembered for certain was the doctor's grim expression as he'd told her it was unlikely she would ever carry a child to term, that it would be best if she didn't try.

Julia hid her face in her arms and wept for the babies she would never hold.

The barnyard was empty and too quiet without Julia and Bandit around. It surprised Hugh that he found it so. He was a man who'd learned to be comfortable with his own company and with silence. Solitude suited him. Only it didn't suit him today.

He'd seen Julia ride out earlier, a rolled blanket secured behind her saddle, Bandit running on ahead of horse and rider as usual. Hugh had wanted to call after her, to ask where she was going, but he'd stopped himself. It wasn't his business. If she'd wanted him to know, she would have told him.

As morning became midday and Julia hadn't returned, hunger drew Hugh into the house to find something to eat. With a sharp knife, he cut himself a couple of slices of bread and several more of cheese. As he nibbled on the latter, he allowed his gaze to roam over the living area until it rested on the chair near the window. He pictured her seated there, sunlight gilding her hair, as he'd seen her a few days before. A different kind of hunger stirred inside of him, a desire to be the kind of man a woman like Julia Grace could look up to.

He might as well wish for the moon.

With a slow shake of his head, he moved toward the open front door. He was stepping onto the porch when a man rode into the barnyard.

The newcomer looked surprised when he saw Hugh. "Mrs. Grace around?" he asked, a note of suspicion in his tone.

"No, she's not."

Who're you? the other man's eyes demanded.

Hugh answered the unspoken question. "I work for Mrs. Grace. Can I help you?"

"My name's Peter Collins. We're her neighbors."

"That's my nearest neighbor's place," Hugh remembered Julia saying. *"The Collins' family. They've got ten children. All girls."*

Ten daughters, huh? No wonder the man had a slightly harried look about him.

"My wife sent me to ask Mrs. Grace to join us for dinner next Sunday. My brother-in-law's coming to visit for a week or two, and Rose would like the two of them to meet. I'd be obliged if you'd tell her when she gets back."

Before Hugh could respond, Bandit ran into the barnyard. The two men looked beyond the corral and paddock and watched as Julia loped her horse toward them. A minute later, she slowed the gelding to a walk and then came to a halt.

"Peter!" A smile of welcome brightened her face. "What brings you to Sage-hen? How're Rose and the girls?"

"They're all fine."

"And the baby?"

"Growing like a weed. Prettiest baby in the world."

Hugh saw a shadow flit across Julia's face.

"Care for a cup of coffee?" She slipped from the saddle and looped the reins around the top rail of the corral.

"Don't mind if I do."

Julia looked at Hugh, her eyes sliding to the remainder of the bread and cheese in his right hand.

"Hope you don't mind that I helped myself," he said. "I got hungry and wasn't sure when you'd be back."

"I don't mind. Only I promised good vittles when I offered you the job, and I don't think bread and cheese measures up."

There were times in his life when the food he held in his hand would have been considered a feast, but she didn't need to know that.

"Come on," she said. "The both of you. Come inside."

Peter dismounted and secured his horse. Hugh waited on the porch, then followed Peter into the house. Julia was already setting the coffeepot on the stove by the time the two men sat at the kitchen table.

"What brings you to Sage-hen, Peter?"

"Rose sent me to ask you to dinner next Sunday." His gaze shifted to Hugh. "Your hired man too, if he wants to come. The more the merrier, like they say." He held out his hand. "Sorry. I didn't get your name when we met outside."

"Hugh Brennan."

The two men shook hands.

"Pleasure," Peter said. "I guess that was you I saw with Julia on your way to town last week."

Hugh nodded.

"You'll be staying on?"

Julia answered before Hugh could. "Just until

after I take the cows to market. Mr. Brennan is on his way to Idaho."

"Oh? Sorry to hear that." Peter turned his gaze from Hugh to Julia. "You could use some help here year 'round."

"Can't afford it," she answered with a patient smile. "But never mind that. What can I bring when we come for Sunday dinner?"

Peter chuckled, obviously knowing when a woman wanted to change a subject. "Not a thing. Rose has got it all planned out, and you know how she is. Likes to do things her own way."

Smiling, Julia settled onto a chair. "Yes, I know."

This was the most relaxed and at ease Hugh had seen Julia since the first day he rode in. That she and Peter were trusted friends was apparent, and it made Hugh feel envious.

Looking at Peter, he said, "Are you sure your wife will want me included? I don't mind if—"

"She'll want you. Rose loves herself a chance to sit down with other adults. More than just me, that is. Most days she's surrounded by a bunch of little ones, so she does love havin' company."

Julia laughed along with Peter, and the companionable mood inside the kitchen chased away the envy and began to warm the lonely places in Hugh's heart.

Peter hadn't lied when he said Rose liked to have company over, but he might have stretched the truth about her being glad to have Hugh Brennan join them. Not when his wife's purpose for the Sunday dinner was to introduce her brother to Julia. Rose was a romantic, and she had matchmaking in mind. Peter had tried to tell her she was wasting her time. Julia Grace wouldn't be interested in his brother-in-law. She wouldn't be interested in another marriage to anyone. Not any time soon, at least.

His gaze shifted to Julia's hired hand. Hugh Brennan was a difficult man to read. There was a wariness that never left his eyes. Even when he laughed, he held something back, as if he didn't quite trust the others at the table. Still, Peter found himself liking the younger man. His wife said he had the gift of discernment. He hoped she was right. His instincts at the moment said there was no reason to wish Hugh gone from Sage-hen.

Julia's next words jerked him from his thoughts. "I reckon Abigail will be getting engaged soon."

"Engaged?" Peter felt his eyes go wide. "Who to?"

She was silent a moment and then laughed again. "Are you telling me you haven't noticed the Kittson boy coming round your place all spring?"

"Mark Kittson? He's been helping me with the planting. I'm paying him to be there."

Julia shook her head, the laughter remaining in her eyes. He knew the look. Rose gave him the same one when she thought him obtuse.

Come to think of it, maybe he was being obtuse about Mark. The boy did tend to spend a lot of time hanging around the front porch before he left for home at day's end. And Abigail did always seem to be present. But engaged? She was too young for that. Just seventeen.

Seventeen. That's how old Rose was when he'd asked her to marry him.

"Great Scott," he whispered beneath his breath.

Julia was still smiling as she waved goodbye to her neighbor before he rode out of sight. His visit had been the perfect tonic for her sagging spirits. And it would be good to spend an afternoon with the Collins family.

I keep to myself too much.

It wasn't easy to break a habit honed by years of practice. Julia had become used to sticking close to home, not socializing with her neighbors, staying inside the borders set for her by her husband. She'd only been able to become friends with Rose because Rose hadn't been cowed by Angus. Rose had driven her wagon into the yard, every year or two with another daughter in tow, and plopped herself down for a visit, ignoring the scowls Angus sent her way.

Bless you, Rose Collins.

"Julia."

She turned toward Hugh, who had exited the house behind her.

"You sure I should go with you next week? I know Mr. Collins didn't come here meaning to ask anyone but you."

"Peter was right. Rose will be delighted to have you come. Besides, I want you to meet her. You'll like her a great deal. Everyone does."

Hugh glanced in the direction of the road, his expression thoughtful. Silence stretched between them, and Julia thought their conversation was at an end. But before she could walk away, he said, "Would you mind telling me something?" He looked at her again. But it was more than just looking. He seemed to *see* her.

"If I can."

"What made you change your mind about me?"

"Change my mind?"

"When I rode in ten days ago, you were wishing you had your rifle to point at me. Now you've got me working here and eating at your table and calling you by your Christian name. Why? You don't know me from Adam."

He was right, of course. She didn't know much about him beyond his name and his willingness to work hard. Yet she wasn't sorry that she'd asked him to stay on. "I'm not sure why," she answered at last.

He studied her with his dark eyes, as if trying to see beyond her words to a truth she didn't know herself.

Suddenly uncomfortable, she turned and stepped off the porch. "I'd best take care of Teddy." She walked toward the gelding, putting an abrupt end on the conversation.

Ten

Hugh could ride a horse as well as most and he could shoot a rifle with some accuracy. However, he was by no stretch of the imagination a cowboy. Still he thought he could take to the life of a cattle rancher. There was something satisfying about getting up with the chickens, eating a hearty breakfast, and then riding out to check the fences and irrigate the land where the cattle grazed. There was something good about falling into bed at night, exhausted but knowing he'd done what he'd been hired to do. Maybe he wouldn't feel the same way after a month. Maybe he'd be more than ready to move on. But for the present, as his second week on the ranch drew to a close, he was glad to be working and living on Sage-hen.

The afternoon had grown surprisingly warm by the time Hugh rode his horse into the barnyard on Wednesday. Sweat trickled down his back, dampening his shirt, and he was in need of a long drink of water to wash down the day's dust.

Julia's horse, Teddy, grazed in the nearby paddock, but Bandit was nowhere to be seen. Unusual. The dog was normally quick to see who had ridden into the yard.

Hugh unsaddled his horse and turned the gelding into the paddock with Teddy. Then he carried the tack into the barn. It was there he found Julia's spaniel, sitting at the bottom of the ladder to the loft, staring upward.

"What is it, fella?" Hugh asked as he set his saddle on the rack. Then he heard Julia's laughter from above.

Bandit whined.

"Julia?"

A few moments passed before she appeared at the top of the ladder. "Come up and see. We have a new litter of kittens."

"I didn't know you had a cat."

"Neither did I." She disappeared from view, her soft laughter trailing behind her.

He couldn't resist climbing the ladder if only to follow that delightful sound. In the corner of the loft, a motley calico cat—her long hair matted —had made a nest for herself in the hay, and a half dozen newborn kittens were attached to the teats on her belly. Julia, kneeling on the floor of the loft, watched them from several feet away.

"I don't know where she came from. She isn't feral, and she doesn't seem to have missed too many meals. She let me pet her, and I even held one of the kittens. They must have been born today."

He knelt beside her. "They look like vermin."

"What a horrid thing to say. They're beautiful."

Beautiful? That was not the term he would use to describe the newborn kittens. Not when they were tiny and hairless and their eyes stuck closed.

"All new life is beautiful," Julia said softly.

He looked at her, saw the sweetness in her expression, seemed to catch a glimpse of her hopes and dreams. *You're the one who's beautiful.*

As if she'd heard his thought, she looked up, their gazes meeting. Her smile slowly faded. He wanted to bring it back but didn't know how.

She looked away. "Don't you like cats, Hugh?" Her voice sounded strained.

"They're all right." He'd have liked a cat in his prison cell, if only to keep down the population of rats and mice, but he couldn't tell her that. "Can't say as I was ever around them much."

"I had a cat when I was young. A stray that I found rummaging in the garbage behind the house where my mother and I lived."

You like to take in strays, don't you, Julia? Alley cats. Thirsty strangers on horseback.

Once again, she seemed to know what he was thinking. Her gaze returned to rest upon him, and in her eyes he saw the compassion she felt for any of God's creatures in need. She'd befriended him as she'd befriended this cat and her kittens.

Except Hugh didn't have friends. Hadn't had a

friend since he was a boy. Then he'd had friends. Lots of them. Boys his own age who'd gotten into mischief with him, who'd teased their sisters just like he'd teased his own, who'd grown too tall for their pants the same way he had that last year before his mum died.

At the memory, regret slammed into him. Regret for the innocence lost that could never be recovered. Regret for the life that might have been but could no longer be. If there was one thing he could undo about his past, he would change the day his father came to that farm in Nebraska. If he had it to do over, he would look Sweeney Brennan straight in the eye and refuse to go back to Chicago with him. Because from the moment he'd left that farm with his dad, he'd traveled a road leading straight to perdition. But how could a boy of fourteen know his own father would betray him in so many ways? Even now, in hindsight, it was hard to believe.

No, a man like Hugh didn't have friends. Especially not a woman as lovely and gentle as Julia Grace.

He got to his feet. "I need to wash up."

"Hugh? Is something—"

"Been a long, hot day." He moved down the ladder and out of her sight.

Julia sat back on her heels, her gaze returning to the cat and kittens. She'd offended Hugh in some way. She was sure of it. There'd been a moment when he looked at her that she'd thought . . . that she'd felt . . .

She shook her head, not wanting to explore what she'd thought or what she'd felt.

"What made you change your mind about me?"

She didn't know the answer to Hugh's question anymore now than she had when he'd asked it. Not really. Maybe her change of mind had been the nudging of the Holy Spirit, an act of compassion. Maybe it had been out of desperation; she'd needed a ranch hand and he'd needed work. Or maybe there was something about Hugh—

Julia stood quickly, more determined than ever to end such thoughts. "You need a bed, kitty. I'll have to find you something."

The cat meowed, as if in agreement, before pulling one of the kittens up to her face and beginning to wash it with her tongue.

Julia climbed down the ladder. Bandit immediately hopped to his feet and came to her side. She stroked his head. "We have seven new members of the family, boy, and you're not to chase any of them. Agreed?"

The dog's gaze was disapproving.

"Come on." Her good mood restored, she laughed and patted his head a second time. "We'd better get supper started."

Bandit understood what that meant—food!— and led the way out of the barn, making straight for the house. But Julia paused as she stepped into the sunlight. Her gaze went to the pump where Hugh was bent over, his head under the stream of cold water gushing from the faucet. Then he straightened and, with both hands, swept his dark hair back from his face. He exuded strength and masculinity as he stood there, water dripping from his face and hair.

A strange sensation gripped her as she watched him. A feeling she couldn't name. A feeling that frightened her by its intensity. He noticed her then. Saw her staring at him. Heat rose up her neck and into her cheeks. She averted her eyes and hurried across the barnyard into the house.

What's wrong with me?

She had learned, early in her marriage, not to make eye contact with other men. Not even to look in their direction if she could help it. It had become habit to keep her gaze locked on the ground a few feet in front of her. Angus had been a jealous man, and it had taken only a little to ignite his anger. A friendly smile from the banker. A nod from the butcher. A word from one of the ranch hands.

But I don't need to be afraid any longer.

She stopped in the middle of the parlor and willed her heart to cease its wild pounding.

Angus can no longer touch me. He can't hurt me. I don't have to live the way I used to live.

She turned toward the open front door, and

even though she couldn't see Hugh Brennan, that same odd feeling fluttered inside of her again. Her world seemed to tilt and spin in a new direction. For years, she'd tamped down her emotions, kept them boxed up, private, secret, even from herself. She'd learned to control her thoughts, her will, her expressions, even her hopes for the future. That hadn't changed much after Angus died. But now?

Something was altering, had already altered, and she feared what that might mean.

Hugh found an empty crate in the far corner of the barn. There were no exposed nails, and it was a good size. Big enough to hold a mother cat and her new brood. With a bit of hay and some old rags, it would make a good bed.

It didn't take long to find the things he needed. Once the crate was ready, he placed it in an empty stall before going up to the loft and bringing the feline family down to ground level, a couple of kittens at a time. "You'll like it down here," he told the cat as she followed him to the ladder on his final trip, the last two kittens in his hands.

She meowed her concern for her offspring before finding her own way down from the loft. By the time Hugh reached the stall, the mother cat was on his heels again.

"You're welcome." He set the kittens in the center of the box with their siblings.

The cat jumped in and did a quick inventory, sniffing each kitten, making certain all were present. Then she lay down and let her kittens begin to nurse once again.

A sound drew Hugh around. There was Julia, a blanket in her arms, about to climb the ladder to the loft.

"They aren't up there," he said, stepping out of the stall.

She stopped, a look of surprise crossing her face. She obviously hadn't seen or heard him.

"I brought them down here." He motioned behind him with his head. "Didn't want to chance them falling out of the loft once they begin to walk."

Julia came to stand beside him, her gaze finding the crate. "You made them a bed."

"Thought it would be more comfortable."

"You brought them down from the loft." She looked at him. "And I was afraid you didn't like cats." A small smile bowed the corners of her mouth. "You're very thoughtful, Mr. Brennan."

Warmed by the compliment more than he wanted to admit to himself, he shrugged.

"I brought a blanket." She held it away from her waist. "Looks like it isn't needed."

"Not yet. But they won't stay confined to that crate for long. Why not leave it nearby?"

"I'll do that." She opened the gate and stepped into the stall.

Hugh watched as she moved straw and hay around, forming a large nest. Then she spread the blanket on top of it before reaching into the box and stroking the cat's head. "I'll bring you some milk and scraps later," she whispered.

She captivated him. With her words. With her smile. With her gentle ways. And whether or not a man like Hugh deserved it, he was glad she felt friendly toward him. Maybe her friendship was offered only because he appeared to be a stray, like that cat, but it didn't matter. He would accept it and return it, for whatever time they were allowed.

Eleven

Julia had worn dark-colored clothes—deep umbers and stony grays—for years before and for many months following her husband's death. She'd chosen them because they so accurately reflected the dark nature of her marriage and her life. But little by little, in the months since Angus died, God had broken through the darkness and begun to heal her by the touch of His Holy Spirit. With that change, she'd started to wear light-colored clothes in different hues, yellows and blues being her favorites.

On this Sunday in May, she pulled a fawn-colored split riding skirt from the wardrobe, along with a robin's-egg-blue blouse. Both had been gifts from Rose, but they'd never been worn. Her friend's dinner seemed the right occasion to change that.

When she stepped outside at the appointed hour, she found Teddy and Hugh's horse saddled and bridled. Hugh stood nearby, handsome in dark wool trousers and a white shirt—neither of them new and both badly wrinkled, no doubt from being stuffed in a saddlebag for more than thirteen hundred miles. His boots had been shined and his hat brushed clean.

He showed one of his brief smiles when he saw her. Then he led the horses toward her, and as he passed Teddy's reins into her outstretched hand, he said, "You look mighty pretty, Julia."

"Thanks," she answered softly. But she hadn't worn the new outfit to catch his notice. Had she? In all honesty, she couldn't say for sure. What she did know was that she was drawn to this man, despite her past and despite knowing so little about him.

Hugh swung into the saddle, and she did the same. They turned their horses and rode away from the house. It wasn't until they'd reached the main road that Hugh broke the lengthy silence.

"Julia."

"Yes."

"I'll be meeting the Collins children. Maybe I should know their names so I don't insult anybody."

His comment caused her to smile. "Peter and Rose wouldn't think ill of you if you couldn't remember or if you mixed them up. It's easy to do. Even I do it on occasion."

"All the same . . ." He looked over at her, waiting.

"They seem to be working their way through the alphabet. That's the easiest way to remember them. And every name is taken from the Bible. Starting with the oldest, there's Abigail, Bathshua, Charity, Dinah, Eden, Faith, Gomer, Hope, India, and Jemima, the baby, who I call Jem."

Hugh released a soft whistle. "I'm doomed."

Laughter burbled up in Julia's chest. "When I can't remember who is who, I simply call them 'girls.' They answer to that well enough."

"Mum sometimes did the same with my sisters, and there were only two of them."

She was pleased that he'd chosen to share something about himself without her asking. "I always wished I'd had a sister."

"It was okay . . . most of the time."

Julia caught a glimpse of the boy he must have been—happy, eager, without a care in the world. "And where are they now? Your sisters."

He gave his head a slow shake, his smile disappearing. "Not sure. Felicia, she's the older of the two, she's supposed to be in a town near Boise City. Diana is the youngest. I don't know for sure where she is. Montana was the last known location but that was a lot of years ago." He squinted up at the sun. "Our mum died when we were kids, and we got separated soon after, placed out with families in the West. Now I'm set on finding them."

It was an abundance of information from a man who had said little about himself over the past two-and-a-half weeks. Julia found herself wanting to know even more. Why had it taken him so long to begin searching for his sisters? Where had he grown up? Had he had a good childhood despite losing his mother at a young age?

She swallowed the questions. She would let him keep his secrets so she could keep hers.

In Rose's opinion, her brother, Roland March, looked every bit the successful attorney that he was in his suit and starched collar. He hadn't changed out of his Sunday best when they returned from church, and she was glad of it. She wanted him to look good for company. Well, to be honest, she wanted him to look good for Julia.

Except for Peter, Rose didn't know as good a man as her big brother. He was kind and generous and honest. He had a successful law practice in Portland, Oregon. While some might not go so far as calling him handsome, he had a pleasant face. If he had a fault, it was that he was too . . . mundane . . . for his own good. At least that was true when it came to matters of the heart. He could argue fine points of the law with the best of them, but his rare attempts at making small talk with young women failed miserably.

Now that their parents had both passed on, Rose wanted to see her brother married. She hated the thought of him living out his days alone in that fine, big house that fairly begged for a large family to fill its many rooms. And she couldn't think of a better wife for him than her dear friend Julia.

Out of the corner of her eye, she caught Peter watching her. *Don't meddle,* his gaze warned. She gave her head a subtle shake before turning and walking into the kitchen.

She checked the ham in the oven. Honey-baked to perfection, if she did say so herself. Along with the ham, she'd be serving potatoes, carrots with onions, rolls with butter and jam, and for dessert, two kinds of pie. People said she made the best pies in the county. And who was she to argue with popular opinion?

Oh, mercy. Pride went before a fall. She'd best remember that.

It was obvious to Hugh—judging by the Collins house—that its owners hadn't planned on a family of ten children. Additional rooms had been added onto the original structure as they'd become necessary, giving the house a sprawling, hodge-podge appearance. The outbuildings, on the other hand, were laid out in an orderly fashion, and from the look of them, all had recently received a fresh coat of paint.

As Hugh and Julia approached, a woman stepped onto the front porch, a baby in arms and a toddler clinging to her skirt. She smiled and waved with her free hand. This, he knew, must be Rose Collins.

Julia stopped her horse and slipped to the ground. Dropping the reins, she climbed the porch steps and hugged her friend's neck. But the moment Julia released Rose, she took the baby into her arms.

"You must be Mr. Brennan," Rose said, looking his way.

"Yes, ma'am." He tugged the brim of his hat before dismounting. "Thanks for having me."

"Glad to have you. You can turn your horses loose in there." She pointed toward a corral. "Come on inside when you're done."

As he reached for Teddy's reins, Hugh glanced once again at Julia, and the expression on her face as she beheld the baby in her arms stole his breath. The longing he saw there forced him to turn away, overcome by the ache it caused in his heart. Julia was almost as careful about not revealing her inner thoughts as he was his own, and he knew she wouldn't like that he'd seen how much she yearned for a baby.

It didn't take long to remove the saddles and

bridles from the horses and turn them loose in the small enclosure. By the time he walked toward the house, the women and little ones had gone inside. Hugh climbed the steps and stopped in the open doorway.

Peter Collins might not have planned enough bedrooms when he first built this house, but he'd given his wife a spacious kitchen. A good thing since much of it was taken up by a long table. Benches lined the long sides. A chair sat at each end.

At this moment, the room buzzed with activity. Several of the elder daughters were setting the table with plates and utensils and drinking glasses. The tallest—and presumably oldest—stirred something in a pot on the stove. The toddler he'd seen earlier on the porch now sat in a corner with some blocks of wood, overseen by a sister of nine or ten years.

"Mr. Brennan," Peter called to him from the parlor to his right. "Come and join us."

Hugh turned in that direction. Julia was seated in a rocking chair, the infant still in her arms. Peter and Rose Collins stood nearby. And the man on the sofa had to be the visiting brother.

Peter shook Hugh's hand, then drew him across the parlor. "Mr. Brennan, this is my wife's brother, Roland March. He's an attorney in Portland, Oregon. Roland, Hugh Brennan. He works on Julia's ranch."

After shaking Roland's hand, Hugh moved to stand near the window, but his gaze was drawn once more to Julia and the baby. It was a sight that made him want to rejoice and weep at the same time. The depth of feelings made him uneasy. They would make Julia uneasy too.

Clearing his throat, he turned toward the window. "You've got a nice spread, Collins. What sort of crops do you grow?"

"Mostly corn, barley, and hay. You interested in farming? I'll be glad to show you around the place."

"Thanks. I'd like to see it." Anything to take him away from Julia long enough for sanity to return.

Julia didn't take her eyes off Jemima for more than an instant. Not until the baby demanded—with strong lungs—to be fed.

"I'll just go into the bedroom," Rose said as she took the infant from Julia. "By the time she's done, we should be ready to sit down to eat too." She motioned with her head toward her brother. "You two make yourself acquainted. I'll be back soon enough."

Julia felt a moment of panic. Rose had introduced her brother upon Julia's arrival, but for the life of her, she couldn't remember his name now.

It was Faith who came to her rescue. "Uncle Roland? Can you get my doll? Charity put it on top of the cupboard, and I can't reach it."

Roland . . . Roland March. That was his name. The panic subsided.

"Excuse me, Mrs. Grace," he said as he rose from the sofa.

She watched as he crossed the parlor and entered the kitchen. He was a tall man and had no trouble retrieving the doll where Faith's sister had tried to hide it. When he turned around, his gaze met Julia's and he smiled.

And in that moment, Julia realized what her friend had in mind. How could she not have known it before now? Rose, who was so happily wed, wanted the same for everyone—and she thought her brother would make some woman a fine husband. Hadn't she said those very words to Julia in the past?

Oh, Rose. I thought you understood how I felt.

It didn't matter that Roland March was nothing like Angus. Julia had no interest in giving over her life to another husband. Not even if she could have a baby would she marry again—and it did not seem to be the Lord's will for her to be a mother.

The Collins family was a boisterous bunch, and the meal that Sunday was anything but silent. Frequent laughter punctured the air as bowls and platters were passed in a circle, older children aiding the younger ones, several conversations taking place at the same time. Hugh had some fond memories of his boyhood with his mum and sisters around the table in their tenement apartment, but those memories were nothing like what he experienced now. In truth, the cacophony was a bit overwhelming for a man who'd spent many of his adult years in solitude.

Julia was the only one at the table who was as quiet as Hugh, and something in her expression told him she was troubled by her own thoughts. Was it because she no longer held the baby in her arms or was it something else? He wished he knew.

"Mr. Brennan," Roland said from his place directly across the table, "my sister tells me you're from Illinois."

"Yes. I grew up in Chicago."

"How long have you been in Wyoming?"

"Not long. Just came here this spring."

"So you haven't always been a cowboy?"

Hugh had met a fair number of lawyers over the years. A necessary evil, he supposed. Most attorneys were brilliant actors even if not brilliant thinkers. And none he'd met had cared about his innocence. When he'd been innocent. He tried not to let his opinion of those in the legal profession reveal itself in his abrupt answer. "No."

"And what sort of profession did you practice in Chicago?"

An image of steel bars flashed in his mind, and he felt himself tense. He didn't want to lie, but he didn't want to tell the whole truth either. His past was none of this man's business. He'd put it behind him, as best he could. It was better forgotten—if that would ever be possible. "Nothing special. Any work I could find."

"Mr. Brennan seems to be skilled at whatever he's asked to do," Julia said softly, her eyes fixed on her plate as she moved food around with her fork without taking a bite.

It surprised Hugh, the way her simple words of praise made him feel. More of a man. Less of a failure. The tension drained from his shoulders, and he felt himself being drawn into the warm circle of friends seated around the table.

Twelve

There was a lightness in Hugh's chest on Monday morning as he rode once again toward the neighboring farm. The feeling had begun around the Collins supper table and persisted even after he and Julia returned to Sage-hen. Was it a sense of belonging or of purpose or of hope? Maybe all three.

Not even a week ago, he'd been convinced that a man like him didn't have friends, but this morning, he could believe he already had a friend or two right here in Wyoming. God said he was a new creation in Christ. Maybe there were good folks here on earth who would see that new creation and overlook his unsavory past. Good folks like Peter and Rose Collins. The salt of the earth. That's what his mum would've called them.

Peter was standing on the front porch when Hugh rode into the barnyard. He waved an arm and called out, "Mornin', Hugh."

"Morning."

"I sure appreciate your offer to help pull those stumps."

"Glad to do it." Hugh stopped his horse and dismounted.

"My brother-in-law had to go into town to take care of some business, but if he gets back in time, he'll join us." Peter held up the cup in his hand. "Want some coffee before we get started?"

"No thanks. Had plenty with my breakfast."

"All right then." Peter set the cup on the porch rail. "You can put your horse in the corral while I get the team."

A short while later, the two men headed off on foot. Hugh carried a couple of shovels and an ax. Peter held a saw in one hand while he led the pair of horses with his other. Neither man spoke, the only sound the soft jangle of harnesses. But once they arrived at the new field, Peter explained that he planned to plant more corn in this section of land. Only first he had to get rid of the half dozen stumps that dotted the field.

"I chopped down the trees last fall. Maples. They've got taproots that grow straight down deep. Been meaning to get the field cleared ever since the snow melted but there just never seemed to be enough time, what with the new baby and all."

"Tell me where to start, and we'll get it done."

"We'll need to dig a trench around the base first." Peter motioned toward the nearest stump. "Any small roots we find have to be cut and removed, and we've got to go deep enough beneath the tree to cut the taproot with the saw. Once it's severed, we'll put a chain around the stump and let the horses pull it out."

Hugh set down the ax before handing the second shovel to Peter. Then the two of them got to work, each taking a different stump. The ground was hard and resisted every jab of the shovel. They would be lucky, Hugh decided, to get half of them removed in a single day.

Julia dried the last of the breakfast dishes and put them away. Afterward, she went outside and stood on the porch, listening to the sounds of morning. The cackling of the hens. The swish of horses' tails. The soft applause of leaves as a breeze swayed the branches.

Peaceful. Quiet.

Lonely.

Lonely?

Miles away, the train whistle blew. A faint but mournful sound. A lonely sound.

But she *wasn't* lonely. She had what she wanted—a warm house, plenty of food, and land upon which to raise her cattle. She was no longer subject to a husband who abused or ridiculed her. She had a faithful dog as a companion and a new family of cats to eventually rid her barn of small rodents.

And Hugh?

Her gaze moved toward the road, as if she expected to still be able to see him. Of course she couldn't. He'd left as soon as he finished breakfast. Gone to help Peter clear a field of tree stumps. It had been good of him to volunteer yesterday. Neighborly.

Like he belongs here.

She closed her eyes. What was the matter with her this morning? Maybe it was that she didn't have enough to do. In the time he'd worked for her, Hugh had taken over many tasks she used to do herself. If idleness was the cause of her confused feelings and thoughts, then she would be glad when it was time for him to move on.

With a shake of her head, she went back inside. Now would be a good time to do some much needed mending. In her bedroom, she settled on the chair near the window and reached into her sewing basket for the skirt with the torn hem.

Although Julia liked to sew new clothes well

enough, mending was one of her least favorite tasks. Perhaps that was because it had been one of her chores from a very early age. She could still recall the scent of her mother's cologne as she'd leaned over Julia's shoulder and showed her how to make almost invisible stitches in the colorful fabrics.

"Oh, Mama," she whispered. "How I wish you would write to me. How I wish you would forgive me."

She sighed, her mending forgotten.

"Julia Crane, is that you?"

Julia felt her insides grow tense as she turned to face Madame Rousseau. "Yes'm."

"Come over here. As I live and breathe, you've blossomed over the summer. I never expected you to turn out so pretty."

Julia's mother had told her time and again to stay out of sight of the woman who owned the saloon. At fourteen, Julia was old enough to understand why.

Madame Rousseau frowned. "You aren't still staying in my shack near Trouble Creek, are you? What could Madeline be thinking, keeping you hidden away in that horrid place?"

"We like it there," Julia answered, though it was a falsehood. She wasn't happy in that house where the wind blew through as if the walls were fabric instead of wood.

"It won't do. It just won't do."

And it wouldn't do. Not once Madame Rousseau made up her mind for it to change. In less than a week, Julia and her mother were living in a room on the third floor of the saloon. That room became both Julia's home and her prison.

At night the laughter and shouts and what passed for music filtered up the staircase and beneath the closed, locked door, leaving Julia tense and sleepless. And she didn't like to think what concessions her mother made to Madame Rousseau that allowed Julia to live there without working.

Working. A respectable sounding word for a way of life that wasn't.

"Someday it'll be better. Someday it will." Her mother had said those words time and time again through the years. She'd made certain Julia went to school and had told her she must ignore the teasing and cruel words of her classmates. "Study hard. Improve your mind and you can improve your life. Be a lady. Don't wind up like me, my darling girl."

Take me away from here, God. That was Julia's constant prayer. *Please take me away from here.*

Julia's eyes refocused, and with a glance at the clock, she realized she'd been lost in thought for a long while. But her memories wouldn't be denied.

She dropped the skirt into the basket and went to her wardrobe. On the top shelf, within easy reach, was a plain wooden box where she kept a few prized possessions. While Angus lived, she'd hidden the box elsewhere, knowing he would have destroyed it and everything inside when he was in one of his moods.

Julia carried the box to her bed where she opened the lid. On top, there were the letters from her mother, sent during the early years of Julia's marriage, tied in a bundle with a yellow ribbon. In a second bundle were the letters her mother had returned to her unopened. Those were from more recent years. In addition, there was a necklace that her great-grandmother had worn when she left England for America, a small silver cross given to Julia by Reverend Adair at her baptism, and a ring that had belonged to Angus's mother. She picked up the latter object and held it up to catch the light.

Her husband had shown her the ring once, soon after he'd brought Julia to Wyoming as his bride. "It's not worth anything," he'd said at the time. "Cut glass is all it is. But my father gave it to my mother, and she liked it. I don't want you wearing it."

She hadn't cared about the ring. It was rather an ugly thing. Though the glass stone was bright and sparkly, the metal setting reminded her of a gargoyle. Why would any woman want it on her finger? She'd never seen the ring again while Angus lived and had forgotten all about it until she was going through her husband's things several months after his death and discovered it in the back of a dresser drawer, wrapped in a handkerchief.

But the ugly ring wasn't the reason she'd taken the keepsake box from the wardrobe. It was the letters she wanted to see. She reached for the bundled envelopes and untied the yellow ribbon. Then she opened the letter with the oldest postmark.

My darling girl,

I hope this letter finds you well and settling into your new life with your husband. I have thought of you so often since the day of the wedding. I know it was not the kind of ceremony you would have liked. I know you would have chosen a church wedding performed by the reverend, but that just wasn't possible. It was more important that you marry quickly and go, before Madame Rousseau made it difficult for you to do so.

Still, you were the prettiest bride I've seen in all my born days, and if I believed in God, I'd be thanking Him for giving you a fine husband and a new home.

"Oh, Mama," she whispered, tears blurring her vision. "You were grasping at straws, trying to protect me. But how I wish . . . how I wish . . ."

. . .

"Julia dear, I want you to meet Mr. Grace."

Her mother's words drew Julia's gaze from the dress she was making. She wasn't sure what she expected, but it wasn't the man she saw before her. His attire was plain, the clothes of a working man. However, his face was anything but plain. Never had she seen such a handsome man. Perhaps four or five years older than she, he was tall and fair, his hair even lighter than her own. His eyes were dark blue. When he smiled, she felt her heart flip in response.

"How do you do, Miss Crane?" he said, his voice smooth, like warm honey.

She answered as she'd been taught to do. "I'm well, sir. Thank you." She glanced toward her mother who remained near the open door of the room they shared, wondering why she'd brought Mr. Grace here instead of calling for her to come down.

"Would you mind if I sat?" he asked, already doing so.

Fear fluttered through her. Was this Madame Rousseau's doing? No, it couldn't be. Her mother wouldn't look so pleased if that were the case.

Her gaze returned to Mr. Grace. "I'm afraid I haven't any refreshments to offer you, sir."

"Quite all right. I'm here for a different reason."

"Different reason?"

"Miss Crane, the truth is, I'm here to ask for your hand in marriage."

"Marriage?" Her eyes widened in disbelief. "But we only just met."

He smiled again. "I know more than you think, Julia. When I first saw you in town, I inquired about you. And now we'll become better acquainted. First of all, I'd like you to call me Angus. Would you do that?"

"I—" She glanced toward her mother, who nodded ever so slightly. "I suppose that would be all right . . . Angus."

The wedding took place less than a week later. It was held in Madame Rousseau's private suite on the first floor above the saloon early on a Wednesday morning. All of the girls who worked for Madame Rousseau were there, a few of them attending in satin robes and bedroom slippers. No one seemed to think that strange, not even the justice of the peace who performed the brief ceremony.

In no time at all, Angus and Julia were declared husband and wife. Angus gave his bride a perfunctory kiss on the lips, took hold of her left arm, and propelled her out of the suite, down the stairs, and out onto the boardwalk, where a wagon and team of horses awaited them, Julia's trunk already in the bed.

"Julia," her mother called before Angus could help her up to the wagon seat.

She turned to accept her mother's embrace.

"Be happy. I've done the best by you that I could."

"I know you have, Mama. I'll be happy."

"You'll never have to work in a place like this. You've got a husband and a home. Make the best of it."

"I will."

Her mother looked at Angus. "You treat her good now, you hear?"

He grunted his response.

"You write me as soon as you get to your new home," her mother continued, looking once more at Julia. "You write me as often as you can. I know you'll be busy, learning how to be a proper rancher's wife and all, but just write enough so I'll know you're doing okay."

Tears flooded Julia's eyes as she whispered, "I will, Mama. You write to me too. I . . . I'll miss you."

"Let's go." Angus took hold of her arm again, his grip painfully tight. "We've got a lot of ground to cover before nightfall."

He sounded almost angry, and a flicker of doubt passed through her heart. But it was too late to change things now.

Once again, Hugh slapped the reins against the rumps of the horses as the animals strained forward in the harness. "Giddup there!" They pulled with all of their might, their coats covered with sweat.

"It's starting to move," Peter shouted. "Keep 'em going."

"Hey there. Giddup."

For a few moments longer, everything was as it had been for the past ten minutes, men and horses all doing their jobs. Then the groan and rattle of leather and chains was replaced by a sharper, louder sound. Unexpectedly, the horses broke into a trot, no longer meeting resistance. Hugh was jerked to his knees and the reins soared out of his hands. Completely free now, the team hurried toward the barn.

"What hap—" The question died in Hugh's throat as he looked behind him. Peter was on the ground near the splintered stump, his head bleeding, his eyes closed. "Collins!" Hugh jumped up, rushed to where the injured man lay, and dropped to his knees a second time.

The wound in Peter's head looked both long and deep, although it was hard to be sure of anything because of the blood. Lots and lots of blood. He jerked his shirt loose from his trousers and peeled out of it. Then he pressed the fabric to the wound, hoping to staunch the flow.

"Collins, are you with me?"

The man didn't answer. His eyes didn't flicker or try to open.

Hugh straightened his back and looked toward

the Collins house. Too far away but he shouted anyway. "Mrs. Collins! Rose! Anyone!" No one was in sight. No one came at the sound of his voice.

Looking back at Peter, he lifted the edge of the shirt. The wound continued to bleed. He applied pressure a second time. He'd seen a man die in the prison yard from a head wound. Other prisoners had stood around and watched the life flow right out of the kid without lifting a finger to help. Hugh didn't want Peter to die the same way. Not if he could do something about it.

"Jesus . . . God . . . Help." It wasn't much as prayers went, but it was the best he could do for now.

Peter was a big man and all muscle. He hadn't an ounce of fat on him. Unconscious, it would be dead weight too. Hugh couldn't keep the shirt pressed to his forehead and carry him at the same time, but he couldn't stay here and do nothing either. The horses were long gone. He would have to carry him. He had no other choice.

"Hold on, Collins."

He lifted Peter's head, sliding his bloodstained shirt beneath it. Then he used the sleeves to tie the fabric as tight as possible over the wound. Without added pressure, it didn't do much to stop the flow of blood.

He'd been right about the dead weight. Every muscle in Hugh's body seemed to cry out in objection as he carried Peter across the field toward the farmhouse. More than once he stumbled, the ground uneven beneath his boots. Somehow he managed to stay upright and keep moving forward. He would have tried calling out again if he'd had any spare breath.

After what seemed an eternity, he reached the corral next to the barn. He stopped and braced a shoulder against the fence. "Mrs. Collins!" Winded, his voice didn't carry far. He glanced at Peter. The man's face—where it wasn't hidden by Hugh's shirt or streaked with his own blood— was pale. Hugh pushed off the fence and pressed onward. Just as he reached the first step the front door opened, revealing Rose, the baby in her arms. Her eyes took in Hugh and Peter. And the blood.

"Merciful God," she breathed. "Bring him inside." She led the way to the couple's bedroom at the back of the house. There, Hugh placed Peter on the bed while Rose lay the infant in a nearby cradle. "What happened?" Rose knelt beside the bed and removed the shirt, revealing the wound.

"I'm not sure. The chain broke free of the harness. It must've struck him in the head. Knocked him out cold."

She looked up. "He needs the doctor. My brother's not back from town yet, and the girls—"

"I'll go for him."

"Thanks." Her gaze returned to her husband. "You'll find one of Peter's shirts in the bureau. Second drawer."

Hugh turned, and as he did so, he saw several of the older daughters crowded into the doorway, looking toward the bed with fear in their eyes. He wanted to offer some words of comfort, but he didn't know what to say.

Julia wasn't surprised by her melancholy mood, and she knew it had more to do with what she would do tomorrow than with memories of her mother or of Angus. But she didn't want to think about that now, nor did she want Hugh to know she'd been crying. So she put away the keepsake box, dried her eyes, and washed her face. Then she went to the kitchen to prepare the evening meal.

Supper was just about ready to set on the table when Bandit alerted her to Hugh's return from the Collins farm. She hurried to the door with the intention of telling him to hurry so they could eat, but the sight of Hugh stopped her in her tracks. Shoulders stooped, eyes cast downward, he rode into the yard wearing a shirt that wasn't the same he'd worn at the breakfast table that morning. By the size, she suspected it belonged to Peter. And was that dried blood on his cheek?

"Hugh?" She stepped to the edge of the porch.

He looked at her as he reined in.

"What is it?" She moved down the steps. "What happened?"

"There was an accident." He dismounted slowly.

It *was* dried blood on his cheek. Alarm sounded in her heart. "Are you all right?"

"I'm unharmed. Peter got hurt."

"Peter. What happened? Is it bad?"

"The doctor says he'll be fine. It isn't serious. He said head wounds don't have to be bad to bleed a lot."

Head wounds? Julia opened her mouth to ask for more details, but the weariness she saw in his eyes made her swallow the words unspoken. Instead, she asked, "Have you eaten?"

He shook his head.

"Wash up and go inside. Supper's ready. I'll take care of your horse."

"No, I'll—"

"Please, Hugh. You look about ready to fall over."

He hesitated a moment longer, then nodded. "All right."

"Go ahead and eat. I'll be in straightaway."

She waited until he'd followed her instructions; then she took his horse's reins and led him toward the barn. Only as she began to loosen the cinch did she notice the dried sweat on the gelding's coat. The horse had been ridden far and hard earlier in the day. She suspected Hugh had ridden to town for the doctor. More questions whirled in her mind as she brushed the horse, then saw that he was well-watered before she turned him loose in the paddock.

When Julia went inside at last, she found Hugh at his usual place at the table. His plate had food on it, but he wasn't eating. His head was bowed, his eyes closed. Resting? Praying? Watching him, she sank onto her own chair. After a short while longer, he looked up and met her gaze.

"You'd better eat before everything is completely cold," she said softly.

He picked up his fork but didn't use it. "I saw a man die from a head wound. I thought—" He broke off and shook his head.

"Eat, Hugh. You can tell me about it later."

And as she watched him take a bite, she sent up a prayer of thanksgiving—first, that the doctor had said Peter would be fine, and second— which surprised her a little, how grateful she felt—that the blood she'd seen on Hugh's cheek hadn't been his own.

Thirteen

The next morning, Rose sat on a chair at her husband's bedside while he visited with Julia and Hugh. Peter's back was braced with pillows, and although his coloring was paler than normal and he winced in pain when he laughed, he seemed more himself.

"Doc told me to stay in bed today and to take it easy the rest of the week." Peter glanced at Rose. "I expect Rosie will make sure I do just that, even though I think it's a lot of foolishness. I've got a bit of a headache. That's all."

"You'll do as you're told." Her gaze shifted from her husband to Hugh. "Lord knows what would've happened to him if you hadn't been there to carry him in and then go for the doctor." She'd said the same thing to him more than once, both yesterday before he'd returned to Sage-hen and this morning since he'd arrived with Julia.

Hugh nodded, and Rose suspected he was growing uncomfortable with her profuse thanks. As if to confirm, he looked at Peter and said, "Maybe Mr. March and I could get the last of the stumps pulled while you're laid up."

Rose saw an amused expression flit across her husband's face and knew exactly what he was thinking. Roland was the last man on earth cut out to be a farmer—and would more than likely be useless when it came to stump removal.

"It can wait until I'm up and about," Peter answered.

Hugh said, "I could manage it, now that you've shown me what to do. You just ask and I'll be here."

As he spoke, Julia smiled at him.

Oh, my stars and garters. Will you look at that? Rose knew in that moment that Roland didn't have a prayer of winning Julia's heart.

After their return from the Collins farm, Julia waited until Hugh was mending some harness inside the barn. Then she slipped away without telling him where she was going, riding Teddy to the top of a knoll where a gnarled, misshapen tree shaded two small headstones. The headstones had only a few words written on them. The first read: *Baby Girl, May 30, 1893.* The second read: *Baby Boy, February 4, 1896.*

Her melancholy mood had been forgotten yesterday with the news of Peter's injury. It had been held at bay while they went to visit him this morning. But the sorrow returned as she knelt on the ground and swept away some winter's leaves that still lay upon the graves.

Only two graves. Her third baby had been lost too soon to need a proper burial.

She touched the headstone for her baby girl. If the child had lived, she would have turned six years old this day. Who would she have looked like? Would she have been a happy child? Would her father have treated her well, even though she'd been a girl instead of a boy?

Julia had wanted to name a daughter for her mother. Angus had said no child of his would bear the name of a woman of ill-repute. When

Julia tried to protest, he'd struck her across the mouth, causing her lip to bleed. She hadn't allowed herself to consider baby names after that.

How fragile life was. Peter could have been taken from them yesterday in an instant. Other lives, like her babies, never had a chance.

Why must it be that way?

There had been times in her past when she'd questioned God without end, when she'd demanded answers to her whys. Why could Rose have children so easily? Why was Julia childless? Why were some wives cherished, as Peter cherished Rose? Why had Julia been despised by the man she'd married?

Why is that pot for water and this pot for ashes?

Yes, she still asked the occasional why, but she no longer demanded answers. She'd come to accept that it was the Potter's right to decide how the vessels He formed were used.

She took hold of some weeds growing near the headstone of her stillborn son and yanked them free. "What would you be like today?" she whispered, picturing a boy of three with pudgy legs, running around in the long grasses of the hillside, squealing his pleasure as only little children could.

Julia sighed as she mentally clamped down on her imagination. After the loss of her son, the doctor had said she would never be able to bear

131

children. His words had been confirmed when she'd miscarried later that same year.

A sigh escaped her. She supposed, since she would never marry again, that her barrenness no longer mattered.

I have much to be thankful for, Lord. She looked toward heaven. *Keep me ever mindful of Your goodness and faithfulness. Forgive me when I fret and complain.*

She drew a deep breath and stood once again, then turned in a slow circle. From this knoll, she had a good view of much of Sage-hen Ranch. The fields where they grew hay. The grasslands where the cattle grazed. The simple log house and the sturdy outbuildings. The barn with its newly patched roof. The paddock and corrals for the horses.

Yes, she had much to be thankful for. True, she had known sorrow here, but now this ranch was her sanctuary. She must remember that always.

With another sigh, she walked to where Teddy grazed, took the reins in hand, mounted, and rode down the sloping hillside toward home.

Hugh had heard Julia ride away from the barnyard. He'd left the harness on the work table and walked out of the barn, watching Julia as she rode to a distant knoll. He'd seen her dismount and kneel on the ground. He'd continued to watch until she remounted her horse and rode toward the house. Only then had he gone back to his work in the barn.

Now, after supper, as the sun hung low in the western sky, Hugh arrived at that same knoll in the shadow of a twisted tree. What he found there were gravestones. Two of them. A baby girl and a baby boy, according to the markers. No names on them. Not even last names. But he knew without being told what that surname was—Grace. He only had to remember the look on Julia's face as she'd held the Collins baby to understand. These were her children. Babies born too early to even receive names.

Through many tribulations we enter the kingdom of God.

He hadn't been a believer long, but he'd already learned the truth of that verse. Trials came to the just and the unjust, same as the rains did. Still, Hugh would wish away this particular heartbreak for the beautiful widow who'd given him work and food and shelter. She'd shown him nothing but kindness from the moment he'd ridden into the barnyard, even when she'd been leery of a stranger.

He shouldn't be here. This was a private, sacred place, and he was trespassing.

He turned his horse and rode away but not in the direction of the barn. If he saw her now, he would say something it was better not to say. He would reveal that he knew something she didn't want him to know. And so he rode east, toward the foothills and the copses of pines and birch and aspens. But he didn't see the hills or the trees. His thoughts went back to Illinois, to the day he'd stood over another grave . . .

A bitter taste coated Hugh's tongue. He'd spent so many nights, lying on his bed, practicing what he would say to his father when he saw him again. He'd wanted to ask why his father had betrayed him. How could a man do that to his own son? He'd let hatred boil to the surface more times than he could count in the years he was incarcerated. Sometimes he'd thought that the hatred and the need for answers to his questions were the only way he could survive.

But there would be no answers now. He wouldn't be able to vent his fury. Sweeney Brennan was dead and buried. Had been long before his son finished serving time in prison. Time that should have been Sweeney's to serve.

Hugh didn't know who'd paid for the old man to be buried or the simple headstone etched with his name with the date of his death. It had to have been an act of charity, for Hugh's father never had been able to hang onto money for long.

Now what?

Where was he to go from here? All that awaited him in Chicago was a life of crime. He could tell a quality pearl necklace from dipped. He could easily distinguish between an expensive stone and cut glass. But what use were those skills to a man who wanted to stay out of prison?

God, how I hated him.

With sheer force of will, Hugh dragged his thoughts back from that grave in Illinois, back from the bitter memories that had haunted him for too many years.

God. He looked up as he reined his horse to a stop. *I've hated my father so long. Do I hate him still?*

He didn't hear a voice, but he knew the answer anyway. Yes, there were remnants of hate still lingering in his heart. And as surely as iron bars, hate would keep him imprisoned. If he wanted to be truly free, he would have to forgive Sweeney Brennan. Forgive it all.

"Help me, Lord. I can't do this alone."

Fourteen

Since neither Hugh nor Julia were experts with a rope, the branding of the calves took at least three times as long as it would have with experienced cowpokes in charge.

It was late on Wednesday afternoon, and Julia was weary beyond description. Sweat under her arms and along her spine caused her blouse to cling to her skin. Too much time in the saddle had made her backside numb. The muscles in her arms burned from the strain of wrestling with calves, some that weighed more than she did.

With an eye on the lowering sun, she took the iron from the fire and walked to where Hugh held down a calf. She paused, drew a breath to steady herself—oh, how she hated the smell of burning hair and flesh—and pressed downward on the hot iron. A few seconds later, the squalling calf was back on its feet and racing toward its mother.

Hugh stood. "You look about ready to topple over. Maybe we should finish up tomorrow."

"I'm all right." She wiped her forearm across her forehead. "There's not that many more to do. I'd just as soon be done with it today."

"Whatever you say." He strode to his horse and stepped into the saddle. But before he could go in search of the next calf, his gaze lifted beyond her and he pulled back on the reins.

Julia turned. A man rode toward them, coming from the direction of the house. She frowned. Now what? She'd gone all winter without having as many guests as had ridden into her barnyard in the past few weeks. She shaded her eyes, trying to see who this visitor must be. A moment later, she recognized him. Sheriff Noonan. What on earth could bring him out this far from town? It couldn't be good.

"Mrs. Grace," he greeted her.

"Sheriff."

Lance Noonan's gaze moved to the cattle. "Busy branding, I see."

"Yes. I plan to drive some of the herd down to the Double T soon."

He looked at her again. "You seem to have managed all right over the winter."

"Did the best I could."

He removed his hat and slid the brim in circles between his fingers. He appeared unsettled, and although Julia couldn't claim to know the man well, it did seem out of character for him.

"Is there something you needed, sheriff?"

"I . . . uh . . . it's been made my unhappy job to inform folks out this way that the county land board's voted to raise taxes."

Alarm leapt in her chest. "How much more?"

"Some have doubled, I was told."

Her heart plummeted. "Doubled?"

She turned her head, her eyes going to Hugh where he sat waiting on horseback. He must have seen the panic in her face, for he immediately nudged his horse and rode toward her. Strange, but having him near helped quiet the fear in her heart. She turned back to the sheriff.

He didn't seem surprised to see Hugh, which meant others in town had been talking about her new hired hand. No surprise there. Gossip rode a fast horse. "Sheriff Noonan, this is Hugh Brennan. Mr. Brennan, this is Sheriff Noonan from Pine Creek."

Hugh dipped his chin in greeting but said nothing.

"Glad to meet you, Mr. Brennan." To Julia he said, "I'd best be headed back to town. It's getting late."

"Thanks for bringing the news."

He set his hat on his head again. "Wish it wasn't more bad news, Mrs. Grace." He remounted his horse, then bid farewell and rode out.

"Bad news?" Hugh asked after a long silence.

"Very bad." *Double the taxes.* The momentary peace vanished and fear came rushing back. She swung into the saddle. "We'll finish the branding tomorrow." Then she cantered Teddy toward the house, her heartbeat racing faster than the horse's hooves.

Teddy had barely stopped before she slipped from the saddle, taking only a moment to wrap the reins around a rail of the corral. Then she hurried into the house and into her bedroom.

Unlike the simple box that held her keepsakes, the money box was made of metal, had a lock and key, and was hidden from view. A real thief would find it easily enough, she supposed, but thieves weren't her problem. Money was. Her taxes raised and possibly doubled!

After taking the money box from the drawer, she set it on the bed, unlocked it, and opened the lid. Inside was what little cash she had left. The sale of the cattle would bring enough to pay what she'd expected her taxes to be and to see her through the coming year. The only way to pay the higher taxes would be to sell more of the cattle. But a rancher could only cull a herd so much before they started losing ground, before the cows couldn't produce enough calves to sell in future years. How long could she hang on? Until the next tax payment was due? Until the one after that? And what if her taxes were tripled next time?

Lord, what am I to do? I don't know enough. I'm not smart enough. When will this end?

Hugh's first instinct when he saw the sheriff was to throw his few belongings into his saddlebags, turn his horse west, and start riding. Fast. As with attorneys, he didn't find much to like about most lawmen. But Sheriff Noonan's bad news had been for Julia, not him, and the lawman hadn't seemed much interested in the hired man. Which suited Hugh fine.

After the sheriff left and Julia returned to the house, Hugh dismounted and kicked dirt on the branding fire. He waited until the coals cooled before he too rode back to the house. In the barnyard, he found Teddy, still wearing saddle and bridle, tied to the corral. Very unlike Julia not to tend to her animals first thing.

Hugh's unease grew as he walked to the front porch, stopping in the open doorway and calling, "Julia?"

It was a short wait before she appeared. A look of helplessness was stamped on her face, and it tugged at his chest. One more reason he should ride out of here, he supposed, and one more reason that he wouldn't. He knew what it was like to be in trouble with no one to help him. He didn't want her to experience more of the same.

"Is there anything I can do for you?" he asked.

"No. There's nothing. Unless you know something more about cattle ranching than I do." The attempt to laugh off what troubled her fell flat.

" 'Fraid not."

"If you'll put Teddy away for me, I'll get something started for our supper. I fear it'll be plain fare tonight."

He wanted to do more for her than just take care of her horse, although for the life of him, he didn't know what that could be. Might help if she would tell him exactly what bad news the sheriff had brought to her. She must have decided it was none of his business. And it wasn't. He'd best try to remember that.

Hugh took his time with the horses, brushing and rubbing them down, holding the feed bucket and talking to them as they ate their serving of grain. Then he turned them into the paddock north of the barn to graze. Julia's black gelding tossed his head, kicked up his heels, then raced to the end of the pasture where he trotted back and forth along the width of the fence. A short while later, Hugh's horse mimicked Teddy's actions.

There's no place I've been that's prettier than right here. Look at it. His eyes lifted from the paddock and horses to the majestic mountains and trees and a grand expanse of blue overhead. *Lord, this world must've been something in Eden before Adam ate from that tree. Sure must've been something. Too bad we ruined it.*

He turned his back to the fence, leaning against it, and his gaze fell upon the house.

After several weeks on Sage-hen Ranch, he felt comfortable with the chores he performed every day. To his surprise, the work appealed to him. It left him tired at the end of the day, and it gave him a sense of satisfaction, as if he'd accomplished something that mattered. For a man who'd found it nearly impossible to find honest employment after his release from prison, that was a good feeling. But would he feel that way if he was doing the same work for someone other than Julia Grace? He wasn't comfortable with the question. He was even less comfortable with the answer.

Probably not.

Years ago, Hugh had learned to guard his emotions. Nothing good happened to him when someone else was able to see what he felt. But there was something about Julia that made him forget to be careful. It was more than just the

141

desire to keep himself aloof. More even than the protectiveness he felt for her. More . . . but what exactly?

Whatever it was, he'd never felt it before, and he'd lay odds he shouldn't feel it now.

He pushed off the fence and walked into the barn. When his eyes adjusted, he found Bandit lying on the hard-packed dirt floor, just outside of the stall where the cat and kittens resided.

"Bet you're making her nervous, fella."

Bandit sat up, as if to give Hugh a better way to stroke his head.

Another new experience, making friends with this spaniel. As a boy, he'd known other kids who owned dogs, but the Brennans had been too poor for a pet. Hard enough to feed the members of the family without adding an animal to the mix. And a man without a job or roof over his head, as he'd been since his release from prison, had no business owning one either. But it pleased Hugh, all the same, that Bandit had given him his approval. At the thought, he chuckled. He wasn't sure what it said about him, that he was pleased by a dog's acceptance. Maybe that he'd set his standards mighty low.

After a quick glance into the stall at the feline family, Hugh strode toward the house. Once again he paused at the open door. Once again, the mistress of the house was nowhere in sight. "Julia?"

Soft sounds came from the bedroom, then, "Just a moment." He heard something close—a door to the wardrobe? a drawer of the dresser?—and a few moments later Julia came out of the bedroom. "Sorry," she said, flipping the long blond braid over her shoulder. "I'll get started on our supper right now."

"Anything I can do to help?" He meant more than helping with the meal and hoped she might understand that.

"No. I'll call you when it's ready."

There was no getting around it. He'd been dismissed. Again. All right. So be it. She didn't have to clobber him over the head with a skillet to know she didn't want to tell him what worried her.

So why did he have to fight the urge to enter the house, take her in his arms, and promise that everything would be all right?

It frightened Julia, how much she wanted to turn to Hugh for help. But she couldn't. She mustn't. She had to learn to do this on her own. She had to run this ranch without help, make the decisions, no matter how difficult they might be. If she turned to any man now . . . If she turned to *this* man now . . .

She went into the kitchen and put a skillet on the stove. When she looked up again, Hugh was no longer standing in the doorway. That was good.

143

Lately, she didn't seem able to think clearly when he was around. And perhaps that was a far greater danger than the raised taxes on this land.

The taxes.

Would it do any good if she went to the county land board and pleaded her case? No. Probably not. No, she would simply have to sell enough cattle to pay the higher taxes. And she would have to let next year take care of itself.

"Heaven help me."

Fifteen

The more Julia thought about her money problems, the more confused she felt, and as much as she wanted to, she wouldn't allow herself to discuss her concerns with Hugh. She was already counting on him in more ways than she'd intended when she hired him. But she had to get advice from someone, and as had been the case for many years, that someone would be Rose.

At the breakfast table two days later, Julia told Hugh she was going to ride over to see how Peter was doing.

"Mind if I come along? I'd like to get those last stumps removed before he tries to do it himself."

A warm sensation squeezed her heart. This was what one neighbor did for another. She wished . . . She wished . . . What did she wish?

Giving her head a quick shake, she said, "I'm sure Peter will be grateful."

"I'll get the horses saddled." Hugh rose from his chair. "We'll be ready to go when you are."

With determination, Julia closed her mind to the strange, unwelcome feelings she had about Hugh. *I hired him to help take the cattle to market.*

A good reminder. She'd best get the cattle sold and the taxes paid so Hugh Brennan could be on his way. Once he was gone from Sage-hen, she would be able to see things clearly again.

Peter sat in a chair on the front porch, enjoying the morning sunshine while listening to the sounds coming from inside the house where the Collins children were receiving their school instruction from their mother. It was a rare moment when he got to hear his daughters as they sat around the large kitchen table, completing their lessons. Usually he was in the fields or the barn, tending to crops or animals. But the doctor had ordered him not to exert himself for another few days, and Rose was making sure he obeyed.

His Rosie girl could be stubborn as all get out when she took a mind to it. Lord love her.

"Care for some company?" Roland asked from the doorway.

Peter looked at his brother-in-law. "Of course. Join me. I'm just woolgathering."

"Not something you get to do very often."

Roland sat in another porch chair. "But there are better ways to get to do it, I surmise."

Peter released a soft chuckle. "True enough."

"I'm going to miss all of you when I return to Portland. Sorry I have to cut short my visit."

"We'll miss having you here. Rose especially. You know how she dotes on you."

"Do you suppose she'll forgive me for not sweeping the lovely Mrs. Grace off her feet?"

"You knew her intentions?"

"Peter, my sister has been playing match-maker for me since I changed out of short pants. I knew before I came for this visit that she must have someone for me to meet, with the hopes of pairing us off. I just didn't know her name until she arrived for Sunday dinner."

Peter chuckled again. "Rose isn't very subtle, I suppose."

"No, not subtle." Roland laughed with Peter. "And as attractive and nice as Mrs. Grace is, I don't believe she would find pleasure in the kind of life I could give her. Political parties. Society events. Evenings debating the law with friends. She doesn't strike me as the sort who would want any of that."

Peter nodded his agreement.

His brother-in-law's expression sobered. "About the news the sheriff brought yesterday. I want your word that you will let me know if you need help with the increase in taxes."

"Roland, I can't—"

"Your word, Peter. If for no other reason than to put my sister's mind at rest." He leaned forward on his chair. "You are a good provider for your family, and I know you told Rose that you have enough in the bank for the taxes even with the increase. But I have none of the obligations you have. God has blessed me financially. Allow me to be part of your family in this way. Please."

"All right, Roland. You have my word. If the need arises, I will contact you."

The sound of horses drew both men's gazes toward the road.

"Looks like your friends have returned." Roland stood as Julia and Hugh rode into the yard. "Good morning, Mrs. Grace. Mr. Brennan."

"Good morning, Mr. March." Julia dismounted and quickly came onto the porch. "How are you, Peter?"

"I'm doing fine. I don't have a good reason to be sitting here, to tell you the truth, other than Rosie won't let me do otherwise."

Julia glanced over her shoulder. "Hugh's come to clear the last of the stumps."

"No need to do that," Peter said. "It can wait until next week."

"Glad to do it," Hugh answered.

Roland took a step forward. "Perhaps I could be of some assistance."

Peter thought the work might go faster for Hugh without his brother-in-law's help, but he kept that opinion to himself.

Julia hadn't been inside the house long before her friend excused the girls from their studies and sent them outside to play until lunch. Then she poured them each a cup of tea and they settled on chairs at the recently vacated table.

"What's troubling you?" Rose asked in her best no-nonsense voice.

"Did the sheriff come to see you and Peter yesterday?"

"About the taxes? Yes, he came by."

"He said some properties have seen the taxes doubled."

"I know. Peter says we'll be all right, but it's hard not to worry. We have money in the bank, but if we were to have a drought or if Peter were to be injured again or . . ." Rose let her voice trail into silence, then added, "I'm awfully good at worrying, I'm afraid."

Julia looked at her hands, wrapped tightly around the tea cup, as if she expected to choke an answer from it. "So am I." She drew a deep breath and released it, relaxing her grip at the same time. "I have no extra funds in the bank to draw on. The only way to raise enough is to sell more cattle. But I'm afraid of what will happen if I do. Not this year, but next year."

"You know what Peter would tell you."

In unison, both women said, "Don't borrow trouble from tomorrow."

They smiled at each other, although Julia knew hers was a poor attempt.

"Maybe the ladies from the church in Pine Creek could hold a bake sale to help raise money for your taxes."

"A bake sale?" Julia was horrified at the suggestion. "I'd rather not share my business with everyone. Besides, they couldn't raise enough from selling pies and cakes, Rose. And I'm not the only person who must find more money because of the land board's decision."

Rose frowned. "You don't suppose Charlie Prescott had anything to do with this, do you?"

"Charlie? Why would he? His taxes must have gone up too. Anyway, he has nothing to do with the land board."

"He knows all the men on the board, and unlike the rest of us, he can afford an increase. Maybe he's calling in favors."

"You always think the worst of him."

"And you are generous to a fault. He is more like his half-brother than you realize."

Julia shook her head. "I mustn't judge Charlie based upon Angus's actions. Other than pestering me about selling Sage-hen, I have no reason to think ill of him."

"Even demons can masquerade as angels of light," Rose muttered.

A chill shuddered down Julia's spine, her friend's words reminding her of Angus when he'd come courting so long ago. She'd been fooled then. Could she be fooled in the same way again? Was Rose right to distrust Charlie?

A baby's cry reached them from the bedroom. Rose stood. "Sounds like Jemima's awake and hungry. I'd best go feed her. You think on what I said. Just be careful, that's all." She left the kitchen, disappearing into the back of the house.

Silence—an unusual condition in the Collins household—surrounded Julia. At Sage-hen, silence was familiar, comfortable. Here, it felt strange. She rose and went out to the porch.

Peter grinned when he saw her. "You two done jabbering already?"

"We weren't jabbering." She gave him a smile before she sat on the chair next to him. "We *never* jabber."

"Ha!"

Julia turned her eyes toward the distant field. She could see Hugh and Roland, although from the porch she couldn't tell who was who, not with both men bent over shovels.

"Did Rose tell you Roland's going back to Portland tomorrow?"

"No, she didn't mention it." Maybe she *could* tell who was who. Even from a distance, there was something about the way Hugh moved.

"I guess you know she's disappointed things didn't work out the way she wanted."

Julia didn't have to ask what he meant. "Roland is a nice man and I'm sure he'll make some woman a wonderful husband. But that woman could never be me. I'll never marry again."

"I wonder."

"Don't."

"Time has a way of changing us, Julia. And God has a way of healing our wounds, if we let Him."

A part of her believed what Peter said. Another part found it impossible to believe. Of course she knew that God could heal her, but could time and healing change her enough that she would want to marry again?

Surely not.

Her gaze returned to Hugh as he worked in the distance.

Her heart fluttered, and she had the strange sense that God wanted to say something to her— if only she had ears to hear.

Hugh figured he could have accomplished just as much without the lawyer's help as with him. Maybe more. Roland was a good sort, but it was obvious he wasn't used to physical labor. He also wasn't much of a talker. Except when he asked the occasional question, Roland didn't speak, concentrating instead on shoveling dirt and cutting tree roots.

But the verbal silence was broken at long last by a young girl's voice. "How ya doing?"

Hugh looked up. Two of the Collins girls stood a short distance away, holding hands. If he wasn't mistaken, the older one was Dinah and the younger one Gomer. Although it was hard to be sure. The girls all had a strong resemblance to one another. "We're almost ready to pull this stump out. Maybe you should go back to the house. Don't want you getting hurt."

"We won't get too close." Dinah shook her head. "Pa won't care if we watch as long as we don't get too close." She looked toward the house and waved. "See? He knows we're here."

Sure enough, Peter raised an arm and waved in return.

"Pa says those taproots go down really deep," Dinah continued.

Her younger sister tugged on her arm. "What's a taproot?"

Dinah shrugged. "You don't need to know. Just be quiet and watch and don't make trouble."

The girl's comment sent Hugh's thoughts speeding back to Chicago, to a time before his mum died. He could hear himself saying almost the same exact words to his younger sisters. Just be quiet. Just watch. Just stay out of trouble. Just don't bother me. Sometimes he'd hated being

Felicia's and Diana's older brother, having to look out for them. He'd been known to complain loudly to their mother.

Strange, wasn't it? Then he'd wanted to make them go away. Now he hoped to find them, to ascertain that they were doing well, maybe even discover if they had a place for him in their lives.

He sunk the shovel deep into the earth, but his thoughts stayed elsewhere.

According to the folks on that farm in the eastern part of this state, Felicia had become a schoolteacher. It was easy to envision her in that role. She'd always been a bookish sort. She'd always been willing to help other children with their studies.

Two more weeks or so, and he would draw his pay from Julia and be on his way. That was good. It was time to find his sisters. Time to honor the promise to his mum. Time to cut short this growing sense of belonging—on Julia's ranch, with these people he'd begun to think of as friends—when the truth was he didn't belong here, would never belong here, perhaps would never belong anywhere.

"Dinah!" a more mature voice called.

For the second time in a short span of time, Hugh stopped shoveling and looked over his shoulder. Abigail, the oldest of the Collins girls, walked toward her sisters, frowning at them.

"What are you and Hope doing out here?

You're bothering Mr. Brennan and Uncle Roland."

Hope. Not Gomer. He'd have to try to remember that.

"We're not botherin' them." Dinah stuck her chin in the air. "We're stayin' out of the way. Aren't we, Mr. Brennan? Aren't we, Uncle Roland?" She looked from Hugh to her uncle and back again.

Abigail stopped beside her sisters. "I don't care. Besides, Ma says you're to get back to the house and wash up so we can eat lunch." She looked toward the men. "She says you're to both come eat too, and you can finish pulling that last stump after."

Roland set aside his shovel immediately. "I'm ready."

Hugh wanted to say that if they had just another half an hour, they'd be finished and could call it a day. But that option wasn't available to him now. Not unless he wanted to be rude to Rose. Reluctantly, he leaned his shovel against the stump and headed toward the house with the others.

From the parlor window, holding the sleeping infant in her arms, Julia watched Hugh's return to the house, along with Roland and three of the Collins girls. Hugh moved with a confident stride, different now than on the day he'd arrived at

Sage-hen. There was a new air of quiet strength about him that appealed to her. It was a strength that would never be turned on a woman in rage or cruelty. She couldn't say how she knew that to be true. She simply knew it.

Once again she felt that flutter in her chest. Once again she felt God wanted to tell her something. Something about Hugh?

But of course not! What would God wish to say to her about a man who was headed for Idaho in a short while? Hugh would be gone, and she would remain in this valley. She would hold onto Sage-hen somehow and live there to her dying day.

Alone.

"Hurry up, slowpokes." Rose stood in the front doorway, watching the small group as they came near. "The food's growing cold." She looked over at Julia with a smile. "That means you too."

"We came to help out, not to be fed."

Rose laughed. "As if cooking for two more mouths makes a bit of difference in this household. And I'll not have anyone clearing a field on an empty stomach."

Julia smiled and determinedly set her troubled thoughts aside. How could she be with this wonderful, boisterous, generous family and do otherwise?

Sixteen

Julia's respite from worry, found at the meal table with her neighbors, was brief. That night was another restless one. Each time she was about to drift into sleep, she would think about the taxes. Then she would begin to count her cattle again, trying to decide how many she would need to sell and wondering how long she could survive after selling so many.

It was close to two in the morning when she gave up trying to sleep. After rising from the bed, she grabbed a shawl to put around her shoulders and went outside onto the porch. The night air was surprisingly warm for this early in June, and a first-quarter moon frosted the barnyard in a white light. She sank onto a wooden chair and waited for an answer to her worries to present itself.

Timothy Trent, the rancher who'd bought Sage-hen cows for the past nine or ten years, was a fair man. He'd always paid Angus well for the cattle that he then shipped to market with his own. There was no reason to believe he wouldn't give her fair market value this year as he had last. But even if she received top dollar, the herd would have to be cut by more than half if she was to have enough money to pay her taxes.

If any of you lack wisdom, let him ask of God,

that giveth to all men liberally, and upbraideth not; and it shall be given him.

As the Bible verse whispered in her heart, she caught her breath. Had she asked God for wisdom? Or had she been too busy telling the Lord how she expected Him to arrange things for her? What if it was His will for her to leave Sage-hen? Could she accept that? Oh, but surely that wasn't His answer. It *couldn't* be His answer. Not after all she'd gone through. Not now. She'd worked hard and prayed hard. She'd set her mind on rejoicing at all times, on praising Him. She'd tried to do all that He asked of her. Surely she *deserved* to keep the ranch. Surely He would provide the means for her to stay.

How could His will be otherwise? Her babies were buried here. Her only friends lived on the neighboring farm. This ranch had been her home and her world for all of her adult life. How would she survive if forced to leave? She knew no other way to make a living. She had no skills or expertise that would recommend her to an employer.

Like my mother before me.

With that thought came another fear. Fear that she would find herself living as her mother had lived, doing the work her mother had done, perhaps still did.

"There isn't any sin the blood of Christ cannot cover," Reverend Adair had said to ten-year-old

Julia as they sat next to one another in the church pew one weekday afternoon.

Julia squinted as she looked at the minister. "Nothing?"

"Nothing." He leaned toward her. "The only thing that can separate us from God is if we reject the gift of salvation that Christ offers."

That wasn't what her classmates at school had told her. They'd said she was going to hell because her mother worked in the saloon, because her mother did *bad things*. She didn't know what those bad things were, but they must be *very* bad.

Julia hated school. She hated not having any friends. She hated being teased. She hated the way the teacher looked at her, the sour expression on the woman's face, as if she had an awful taste in her mouth. But Mama was determined Julia would go to school, just as she was determined Julia would go to church on Sundays. Mama didn't go to church so she didn't understand that Julia wasn't welcome there either. Leastwise, not by most folks. The reverend, though, was always nice to her.

"Would you like to pray with me, Julia, for Jesus to be your Savior? Would you like to ask God to be your heavenly Father?"

Julia's eyes widened. "He'd do that? I don't have a pa."

"I know." The reverend had smiled. "And yes, He will do that. All you need to do is ask Him."

• • •

Hugh wasn't sure what caused him to awaken, but at least it hadn't been a nightmare. Thankfully, those had grown infrequent in the weeks he'd been at Sage-hen. Perhaps because he fell onto his cot so tired every night. Too tired to dream, good or bad. Or was it this place that gave him peace in the night? Would the nightmares return when he left the ranch in a couple of weeks?

Sitting on the side of his bed, he raked the fingers of both hands through his hair.

It frightened him a little, how at home he felt here. Perhaps because he hadn't felt at home anywhere since his mother passed away nearly two decades ago. A crowded orphanage. A smoky passenger car on a train hurtling west. A stranger's house on the Nebraskan prairie. Abandoned warehouses and rooms that smelled of garlic and sweat and cheap whiskey. A prison cell filled with despair.

And now Sage-hen.

And now Julia Grace. When he was with her, he felt . . . he felt . . . What? Like more of a man. Like a better man. Or at least like he wanted to be a better man.

He stood, pulled on trousers and shirt, and walked outside, hoping the fresh air would clear his head, rid him of the image of Julia, stop him from wanting . . . more. But instead of escaping thoughts of Julia, he discovered the living, breathing version of the woman.

As had happened once before in the middle of the night, her white nightgown caught the moonlight and gave her presence away. Unlike before, Hugh didn't remain near the barn. He strode toward the house, the earth cool beneath his bare feet. Bandit lay near Julia's chair and didn't bother to rise at Hugh's approach.

"Couldn't sleep?" he asked, stopping without climbing to the porch.

She pulled the dark shawl tighter. "No."

"Me neither." He turned and sat on the top step. "Pretty night."

"Mmm."

He looked upward. "Must be a million stars. Got to look at them through a telescope once." He omitted the part about him being in a man's home to take his valuables and had happened upon the telescope. "It was amazing. Some stars looked close enough to reach out and touch."

Julia rose and walked to the porch railing where she leaned forward and looked up at the night sky. He didn't turn his head, afraid if he did so she might retreat into the house.

After a lengthy silence, she said, "May I ask you something?"

"Sure." He shrugged, not knowing if she looked at him or not. Hopefully, she wouldn't ask anything he wasn't prepared to answer truthfully.

"How did you come to faith in Christ?"

He released a breath. This he could talk about without hesitation. "Reading the Bible." The words were simple enough, the meaning behind them deeper, more profound. "A preacher gave it to me back in Chicago. I didn't have anything else to read on the long trip west, so I read it. I was in Colorado when I began to understand what it was saying. You know. About grace and mercy. Something changed inside of me. Can't explain it. Just know it happened. One minute I wasn't a believer. The next I was. Born again, like Jesus said."

"You don't have to explain it, Hugh. I understand."

Although hospitable and kind, Julia had kept up a barrier between them, a closed door that kept him from getting too close, to keep him from knowing her too well. Hugh couldn't blame her. He had his own doors of protection. All the same, there was something about her words that indicated she'd cracked the door open.

Hugh felt encouraged. "What about you? Did you always believe?"

"No one's born a Christian." Her voice was laced with amusement.

The words caused him to twist on the step and look at her at last. Her long hair cascaded freely over her shoulders, silvered by the moonlight. The hem of the white nightgown brushed her ankles.

Her feet, like his, were bare. For some reason, their bareness made him feel trusted.

She continued, "It was a minister in Grand Coeur where I grew up who told me about Jesus and how He would forgive my sins and that God wanted to be my father. I was sitting here, remembering, before you came out of the barn. I never knew my father, and so to know God would be that for me was very special."

"How old were you when you were born again?"

"Ten."

"Ten. I envy you."

"Why?"

"Maybe if I'd known God in a meaningful way when I was a boy, I wouldn't have made so many mistakes when I was older."

"What sort of mistakes?"

He drew a breath and let it out. "Stupid ones." The two words said a lot and nothing at all, but they were all he was willing to say.

"I've made my share of those," she said softly. "Believing in God doesn't mean we live perfectly, no matter how hard we try."

Even in the darkness of night, he saw a sadness flit across her face that he would do almost anything to wipe away. If it were in his power, he would make certain sorrow was driven out and never approached her life again. But such a thing wasn't in his power. It would never be in his power. Best he remember that.

162

He stood, feigned a yawn, then said, "Guess I'd better try to get some sleep. Dawn'll be here before we know it." He went down the steps. "Night, Julia."

Softly, he heard her return, "Good night, Hugh."

Perhaps it was because she'd told Hugh about Reverend Adair, but Julia couldn't seem to shake memories of her childhood in Grand Coeur. And more specifically, memories of her mother. And so she sat at her writing desk in those wee hours of the morning and wrote another letter, praying with each stroke of the pen that this one wouldn't be returned to her as so many others had been. She prayed her mother would read the letter and answer it and forgive her.

Madeline Crane
Paradise Saloon
Grand Coeur, Idaho

Dear Mother,

It has been over three years since I last wrote to you. Over three years since that same letter was returned to me unopened, like the nine letters sent before it. I do not know if you will decide to read this one, but I have to try one more time. I have to try again to tell you I am sorry for blaming you for the way things used to be. I know you acted out of love for me. I didn't always realize it, but I do now.

Much has changed for me since the last time you received a letter of mine. Angus died more than a year ago. He took sick, running a high fever, then he got pneumonia in his lungs and died. It happened very fast. Just a few days. He was young and strong and no one expected him to die. Not even the doctor from Pine Creek.

Because of the difficulty of my marriage, you might be surprised to learn that I have found contentment at Sage-hen Ranch. Yes, I remember the sad times, especially when I think of the babies I lost, but it was here also that my faith became strong. And so I hope to remain here.

But that may not be possible. The taxes on the ranch are due soon, and while I expect to be able to pay them this year, it may not be possible the next. Angus's brother wants the ranch and has offered to buy it from me, but I do not want to sell, which is probably foolish.

I am not completely alone. There is a man who works for me at present, and there are my neighbors, Peter and Rose Collins. I wrote to you before about them. I am blessed to call them my friends.

What of you, Mother? Five years is such a long time to go without a word. Are you well? Are you still at Madame Rousseau's?

Even if you do not answer this letter, I am praying that you will read it and will forgive me at last for my harsh words written so long ago. I love you, and you are often in my thoughts and prayers.

Your daughter,
Julia Grace

Tears streaked her cheeks by the time she folded the paper and slipped it into an envelope.

"Please, God," she whispered. "Let her read this one. Even if she never writes back, let her know I'm sorry."

Seventeen

When Hugh left his room early Saturday morning, he missed stepping on one of the kittens by a mere inch or two. He wasn't even sure how he saw the tiny orange ball of fur in the dim light.

"Hey there."

He bent down, scooped it up with one hand, and brought it close. Its eyes were still closed, its ears still flattened to its head. He didn't know much about felines, but he knew this one was too young to have made its way out of that stall on its own. It couldn't walk yet. Which meant the mother cat must be relocating her litter.

"You'd think she'd want to stay where there's food and water brought to her every day. Wouldn't you?"

The kitten immediately began its high-pitched meowing. Hugh walked to the stall and looked in. The mother cat was nowhere to be seen, and only one kitten remained in the crate. It too had begun to yowl.

"You guys are sure noisy for being so little."

He opened the stall gate and put the kitten with its sibling. Before he could turn to leave, the mother cat sailed over the top rail of the stall. Her paws landed in the straw, and immediately her back arched as she hissed at Hugh. Before he could react, he heard a soft laugh. A much prettier sound than the one the two kittens were making. And heaven help him, he could get used to the sound of Julia's laughter.

"I don't think she likes you, Hugh." Julia stepped through the open gate. Her face was hidden in shadows, but he could tell by her voice that she was smiling.

"I'm in her way. She's busy moving her kittens."

"Oh no. I was hoping she'd stay put. Where's she taking them?"

"Not sure. She left that little orange one outside the door to my room. I almost stepped on it."

"Ooooh." She knelt in the straw and took up the kitten he'd set down moments before. "You poor baby." She rubbed its back against her cheek. "I hope they'll be all right while we're gone on the cattle drive."

"How soon will we go?"

She looked at him. "We'll plan to begin the drive early on Wednesday. While we're gone, Peter and one of his girls will come over a couple of times a day to see to the chickens and other livestock. And these little guys." She put the kitten in the crate and stood. "If all goes as expected, we should be back by Friday night. Two days going. One to return."

Back by Friday night. Then the work he was doing for her would be done. He should be glad to move on. He wasn't.

As if reading his thoughts, she said, "You'll probably want to give your horse some rest after the drive before you start out on another long trip. But I reckon you can leave by the following Monday."

"Reckon so." Nine days. Nine days and he would leave for Boise City. And he would miss Julia. He would miss seeing her at breakfast each morning and at supper each evening. He would miss her soft laughter and her gentle spirit. He would miss the love he saw in her eyes when she held little Jemima Collins, the tenderness when she cradled the kittens in the palm of her hand. Not that she cared if he would miss her. Not that she should care.

Julia stood and brushed off the straw clinging

to her skirt. "We should start bringing the cattle up closer to the house. Then I can separate the ones going to market from the others. We can get started as soon as we're done with breakfast."

"I'll get the horses saddled."

She nodded, then walked out of the stall.

Nine days wasn't long enough. Not nearly long enough.

Julia had planned to send Hugh one direction while she went another. That way, they could cover more ground and round up more cattle in a shorter amount of time. But after they mounted their horses, Julia found herself reluctant to ride off on her own. No, that wasn't quite true. It was more a wanting to be *with* Hugh.

They loped their horses east, then turned them north when the barbed-wire fence that followed her property line came into view. Another ten minutes, and Hugh drew in on the reins. Julia slowed her horse too but didn't know why. She couldn't see any cattle.

"Look," Hugh said, pointing. "Up there. A section of fence is down."

She followed the direction of his outstretched arm with her eyes, nudging Teddy forward even before she found the problem: barbed wire curled in upon itself between two fence posts. All three strands, broken in the same spot. Even before they got close, she knew this was no accident. The wire had been cut. When they reached the spot, her gaze dropped to the ground. She saw some evidence of the presence of horses but no sign that a large number of cattle had passed through the opening.

"Looks like somebody meant for you to lose some cattle," Hugh said, echoing her thoughts.

"I don't think they got any. The ground doesn't seem to be disturbed."

"Whose property is that?"

"The state owns it." She looked at Hugh. "Let's find where the cows are grazing and get them moved up to the ranch house."

As she nudged Teddy with her heels, Rose's voice whispered in her head, *"You don't suppose Charlie Prescott had anything to do with this, do you?"*

She glanced over her shoulder at the cut wire. Charlie had no reason to steal her cattle or to want them to wander away. Did he?

"He is more like his half-brother than you realize."

Could Rose be right about Charlie? But Julia had no reason to doubt him. He'd never done her any harm. Wasn't judging others wrong? Especially if she painted him with Angus's brush simply because of appearances.

She looked forward again and asked her gelding for more speed. She wouldn't be able to relax again until she'd counted her cows and calves and made certain all were where they belonged.

Small as Sage-hen Ranch was—by Wyoming standards, at least—it still took the better part of the day before Hugh and Julia drove the last of the cattle toward the house. Once there, she sent him to repair the downed fence while she culled the herd. By the time Hugh returned, Julia had managed to separate the cows headed for market from those who would remain on the ranch.

"And the count?" Hugh asked as he began to unsaddle his horse.

"None lost."

"Then my guess is, whoever cut that fence saw us coming and hightailed it into the trees. They didn't have time to steal any of the herd today, but they might try again."

"In all my years on Sage-hen, this is the first time anybody's tampered with the fence or tried to steal the cows. Why now?"

Hugh turned to look at Julia. "You're a woman. Maybe someone thinks that makes you easy pickings."

"Well, I'm *not*." She stiffened her back and jutted out her chin.

He couldn't help it. He chuckled. "I like your courage, Julia Grace. Most men I know don't have your fire and spunk." He wasn't sure how he'd expected her to respond, but it hadn't been the blush that rose in her cheeks.

Something new blossomed inside of him. Not just a need to protect her, to help her. He wanted more. He wanted to kiss her. He wanted her to look up into his eyes and see him as a man, as a *good* man. He wanted her to open her heart to him. He wanted to—

Her eyes widened and her face paled. "I . . . I'd best get us something to eat. Afraid we'll have to make do with cold meat and bread."

"Whatever you fix is fine with me."

She left the barn.

More truthfully, she fled the barn. She fled him. She'd seen the desire in his eyes and had run from him. Could he blame her? Even not knowing the whole truth about him, she had to discern the type of man he'd been, the way he'd lived his life. He wasn't worthy of a woman like her. Jesus had washed him white as snow, but he would still never be good enough for Julia. The past would follow him wherever he went, dragged along like a ball and chain. That was just the way this world was.

He finished tending to the horses and the rest of the livestock, then went to the pump and washed up as best he could before walking to the house. Julia waited for him in the kitchen. She too had washed and changed. She reminded him of a delicate flower blooming in a stark landscape. He

171

longed to draw close and breathe in her beauty, a beauty that was much more than physical. He couldn't, of course, but he wished he could.

Julia motioned to the table, set with a platter holding cold roast beef and slices of cheese and another platter of day-old bread. "You must be starved. It's a long time since we ate our sandwiches."

Yes, he was hungry. But for much more than the food laid out before him. He was hungry for the kind of goodness Julia represented, a goodness he would never have and never deserve. Anger surged through Hugh, hot and unexpected. Anger toward his dad, who had made him a thief and then let him, the son, go to prison for a crime committed by the father. The rage nearly paralyzed him and made him feel even less worthy to sit down at this good woman's supper table than he'd felt already.

"Hugh?"

He shook his head. "Sorry. More tired than I thought." He pulled out a chair for her.

"Thank you," she said softly.

He sat opposite her and waited for her to bless the food, thankful she didn't ask him to do it as she had in the past. They ate in silence. Hugh supposed Julia was too weary to talk. For himself, his mind was too troubled to attempt chitchat.

Lord . . . how do I calm my thoughts? How do I forgive, once and for all?

He looked up from his supper plate. "Could I go with you in the morning?"

"With me?"

Where the idea had come from, he couldn't say. Maybe it had come from God in answer to his prayer. "To your place of worship."

He had asked too much. He could see, in her eyes and in the set of her mouth, that she wanted to refuse him. And yet, when she answered, it was with the grace he had come to expect from her. "Yes. You may come with me."

Eighteen

On Sunday morning, with Bandit leading the way, Julia and Hugh rode out together. Her horse didn't need her to guide him. Teddy had carried her to this place by the river many times over the years, and he always seemed to sense when that was their destination.

Neither of them spoke during the short ride. But when they arrived at the bend of the river and Julia drew back on the reins, Hugh broke the silence. "I see why you like to come here to worship."

Pleasure warmed her heart. Yesterday she'd feared bringing him with her because of all that it meant to her. It was her private sanctuary, a place of intimacy with God, a sacred place. But an unexpected joy welled inside her, to share this special place with someone who could understand, even just a little, what she felt when she came here. Most assuredly Angus wouldn't have understood. Her husband, who had profaned the name of God and mocked her faith, would never have belonged.

Hugh dismounted. Leaving the horse's reins to trail the ground, he walked to the riverbank and stared north. Julia watched him for a short while, then slipped from the saddle, untied the blanket, and spread it on the rock. By the time Hugh turned around, she was settled on it with her Bible open on her lap.

He gave her a tentative smile as he returned to where she sat. "Are you sorry you brought me?"

"No."

"Are you sure? 'Cause I can go if you want me to."

"I don't want you to go." As the answer left her mouth, she feared it might mean something more than just this day and this place. She lowered her eyes quickly to the open book, not wanting Hugh to guess her thoughts.

In silence, he got his own Bible from the saddle bag and joined her on the blanket, keeping a respectable distance.

Not knowing what else to do, she closed her eyes and began to bless the Lord with words from the Psalms, as was her usual practice. "Praise ye the Lord. Praise God in his sanctuary: praise him in the firmament of his power. Praise him for his mighty acts: praise him according to his excellent greatness."

Hugh's voice joined hers. "Praise him with the sound of the trumpet: praise him with the psaltery and harp. Praise him with the timbrel and dance: praise him with stringed instruments and organs."

Looking at the man opposite her, Julia stopped speaking in order to hear him more clearly.

"Praise him upon the loud cymbals: praise him upon the high sounding cymbals. Let every thing that hath breath praise the Lord. Praise ye the Lord." Hugh opened his eyes.

Something softened in her heart as their gazes met and held.

"Psalm 150," he said. "I like that one."

"You've memorized a lot of Scripture in a short time."

He shrugged. "It's a gift, I guess. I remember the things I read. Always have. Been that way since I was a kid." Another small smile curved the corners of his mouth. "I can still quote lines from the storybooks I used to read to my sisters when they were little."

"Your sisters were lucky. I had no one to read to me when I was a child." Something about the way he looked at her—a gentle caring, a lack of judgment—caused her to continue. "I was an only child and my mother . . . worked a lot." She felt embarrassment warming her cheeks. "She wasn't home when I went to bed." Could he see through

175

her carefully chosen words to the sordid truth beyond? What would he think of her if he knew she had no earthly father? Would the way he looked at her change?

"Want to hear one of those children stories?" Hugh asked softly.

Her heart fluttered, and she found she couldn't answer as tears sprang to her eyes.

If he noticed, he didn't let on. "Let's see. Which one did my sisters like best? Ah, yes. I remember." He cleared his throat and schooled his face into a grave expression.

"Croak!" said the toad,
"I'm hungry, I think;
Today I've had nothing
To eat or to drink.

I'll crawl to a garden
And jump through the pales,
And there I'll dine nicely
On slugs and on snails."

"Ho, ho!" quoth the frog,
"Is that what you mean?
Then I'll hop away to
The next meadow stream;

There I will drink, and
Eat worms and slugs too,
And then I shall have a
Good dinner like you."

As Hugh finished the rhyme, he waved his hand in the air with a flourish, then bowed at the waist.

It was all so unexpected, she couldn't help but laugh.

He gave her one of his crooked grins.

Covering her mouth with her hand, she wondered how they had transitioned so quickly from praising God with a psalm to amusement over a children's rhyme about toads and frogs. They had come to this place by the river for church. Was it sacrilege to laugh and be silly? Even as the question drifted into her thoughts, a gust of wind caused the trees to dance, and she would swear she heard God laughing too.

That's how it was supposed to be. Wasn't it? A father laughing over his children, enjoying them. God delighted in her as His daughter. She forgot that so easily. She felt unloved too often. Ashamed of how she'd come to be. Perhaps she forgot because she'd had too few examples in her life of men who were loving and caring. Too few father figures. Reverend Adair had been one of those few. Peter Collins was another.

And perhaps Hugh Brennan?

No, she didn't think of him as a father figure. Her feelings for him were . . . much more complicated.

Her amusement faded away.

· · ·

Hugh saw the laughter leave Julia's eyes. He wanted to bring it back but didn't know how. Not for the first time, the temptation to hold her and kiss her swept over him.

"What sort of man was your father?" she asked into the awkward silence.

Her question caught him unawares. How to answer without revealing more than he wanted? He'd told her bits and pieces of his past. She didn't know of his conviction and imprisonment. He would like to leave it that way. He'd like to move on without her knowing the worst about him. Was that wrong? Could it matter since he was leaving Sage-hen, never to see her again? And yet, the way she looked at him now, it made him want to answer her question.

"He liked his liquor," he said at last.

Her mouth formed a silent *oh,* and something about her expression told him she understood more than he thought she might.

"His name was Sweeney. Sweeney Brennan. Like I said before, he wasn't around much." He released a mirthless chuckle. "Often enough to sire three children, but not much more than that. Our mum took in washing and mending. She did whatever she could to put food on the table for me and my sisters, and she got old long before her time. She took sick and died when I was thirteen."

"I'm sorry, Hugh."

He shrugged. "I never expected to see our dad again, but when he learned we'd been placed out by the orphanage run by Dr. Cray, he came looking for me and took me back to Chicago."

Even at thirteen, Hugh should have known his dad hadn't come for him out of fatherly devotion. Perhaps he had known, deep down in a secret place in his heart, but he'd pretended otherwise. He'd wanted to be with his father, even as Sweeney taught him how to pick pockets and slip into the homes of the wealthy through partially open windows, even as he'd taught him how to tell the difference between worthless trinkets and jewelry that was valuable. Things he knew his mum would disapprove of had she been alive. Hugh had done plenty of bad things, illegal things, during those five years with his father. He'd stolen from the rich and from the not so rich. But he'd never physically hurt anyone. He'd never pulled a knife and stuck it into a man's back.

Sweeney Brennan had done that.

But the law had said otherwise.

Julia reached across the space that separated them and touched the back of his hand with her fingertips. "You needn't tell me anymore. I can see it's painful to remember him." She pulled her hand away again.

Tell her. Tell her the whole truth.

She continued, "I was angry at my mother for a long time. I blamed her for the unhappiness of my marriage. But I finally realized it wasn't her fault. She did the best by me that she could. I understand that now." She turned her eyes toward the river. "Nobody's perfect. We all make mistakes."

Tell her. But he hadn't the courage to obey that small voice in his heart. He hadn't the courage to let her know the kind of man he really was— or at least the kind of man he used to be. Silence stretched between them, the laughter they'd shared earlier forgotten.

At long last, Julia said, "We should go." She stood. "This probably wasn't what you had in mind when you asked to join me here. I'm sorry."

He got to his feet, frustrated by the words locked inside him. He'd waited too long. The opportunity to speak anything that mattered had passed. Maybe that was for the best.

The wagon hit a rut, and Rose grabbed for the edge of the seat to steady herself. Thank goodness they were almost to Pine Creek—and with any luck they would be there before the opening hymn began. Although that didn't mean she approved of Peter being jounced all about. It couldn't be good for his head, even though he insisted he was fine.

Early on in their marriage, Rose and Peter had agreed she would school their daughters at home. The farm was too far from town for the children to make the long trek on foot every week day.

But Peter was adamant that his family wouldn't miss church on Sundays except in the worst of winter weather. He'd been just as adamant this morning.

"Don't say it, Rosie girl."

She glanced to her left. "Don't say what?"

"After all these years, I can tell what you're thinking."

She grunted softly.

"There's nothing ailin' me now that a bit of good preaching won't set right."

Rose pressed her lips together and straightened on the wagon seat. That's when she saw Charlie Prescott, riding toward them. Dislike rose like bile in her throat. He reined in and waited for them to draw closer. When they did, Peter slowed the team to a halt as well.

"Collins." Charlie tipped his hat.

"Prescott," Peter returned with a nod of his head.

"Heard you had an accident."

"Nothing much."

"Heard that fellow Julia's got working for her was the cause of it."

"You heard wrong. The fault was my own."

What does he want? Don't tell him our business. Rose cleared her throat, hoping Peter would take the hint and move the horses along.

"Well, that's good to know. I'd hate to think Julia had someone untrustworthy working on her place. No one in these parts seems to know anything about him."

"His name's Hugh Brennan, and he's from Illinois. He's made no effort to keep that a secret." *At least not from people like Julia or us.*

"Ah. That's right. Brennan from Illinois." Charlie's gaze moved slowly over the girls in the bed of the wagon, then returned to Peter and Rose on the wagon seat. "Well, you take better care of yourself, Collins. I'd hate to think what would happen to your lovely family without you." He tipped his hat again. "Good day to you." Then he rode on.

A chill shivered down Rose's spine. "Peter, I think he was threatening you."

"Now don't go gettin' yourself in a lather, Rosie." He slapped the reins against the team's backsides. "That's just how Charlie Prescott talks. He's full of his own self-importance."

Rose wished she was as confident as her husband sounded.

Nineteen

Julia watched from the doorway of the house as Hugh climbed onto the wagon seat, a strange ache in her heart. It had started yesterday morning by the river. She didn't know what had gone wrong exactly. He'd said a little about his father. She'd said a little about her mother. Nothing that should have caused an uncomfortable silence to settle over them, and yet it had.

And it was that way still.

Julia felt a small hiccup in her heart as she moved off the porch and walked to the wagon. "Here's the list of supplies we'll need. And I've got a letter for you to take to the post office while you're in town." She held out her hand to pass him both items.

He stuffed them into his shirt pocket without glancing at them.

"On the way back, would you mind stopping by to see Peter? Make sure he still feels up to watching the place while we're gone. Remind him we plan to leave Wednesday."

"I'll tell him."

She took a couple of steps back. "Just have Mrs. Humphrey put the supplies on my bill. She'll remember you. Tell her I'll be in next week to pay it in full."

Hugh nodded, then slapped the reins. The wagon jerked into motion.

Her chest hurt as she watched him leave. It would hurt even more when she watched him ride away for good. It was no use pretending that he meant nothing to her. That would be a lie. She liked Hugh. She liked him too much.

"Oh, God. How did I let this happen?"

Bandit rubbed against her leg and she leaned down to stroke his head.

"Don't I have enough trouble without adding this to the mix?"

The dog stared up at her with doleful eyes.

Drawing a deep breath, she straightened. "We'll be all right, won't we, boy? Once I've sold the cattle and paid the taxes and Hugh goes on his way . . ."

Her words trailed into silence. She hadn't the strength to speak them, let alone believe them.

Hugh wasn't long in the mercantile. The list of supplies was a short one. As Julia had expected, Nancy Humphrey remembered him from his first visit to Pine Creek and didn't hesitate to add the items to Julia's account.

Finished in the store, he left the team and wagon in front of the mercantile and followed the boardwalk toward the post office. Almost to his destination, he took the envelope from his pocket, glancing at the address: *Madeline Crane, Grand Coeur, Idaho.* He wondered who—

"Mr. Brennan. We meet again."

Hugh stopped and looked up. Charlie Prescott stood about three yards ahead of him, right outside the post office entrance.

Charlie looked beyond him. "Is Julia with you?"

"No."

"Too bad. I thought I might be saved another trip to talk to her." His gaze returned to Hugh. "You aren't from around here, Brennan, so maybe you aren't aware of this. Julia's in trouble. She doesn't have what it takes to manage that ranch, and she doesn't have the money to hold on to it either. I've tried to make her see that. I've offered to buy the ranch, but she's as stubborn as she is beautiful."

Hugh wanted to grind his teeth. He didn't like Charlie talking about Julia's appearance or her ranch. "She seems to be doing all right."

"Tell Julia I'll be out to see her again soon. After she gets back from the cattle drive. That must be coming up this week. Right?"

Do your own dirty work, Prescott. I'm not your messenger boy. But even as the thought shot through Hugh's mind, he knew he would pass along Charlie Prescott's message as soon as he got back to the ranch. He had to tell her. She needed to know. It wasn't his right to keep things from her.

Charlie chuckled. "Well, at least you're a cow-poke who has the good sense to keep his mouth shut when he should. And yet you're wondering how I know her business. It's easy enough. Angus's cattle got driven to market at the same time every year. It's no secret. Of course she's going to do what my brother did. She wouldn't know to do otherwise."

Hugh wanted nothing more than to punch that self-satisfied smirk off Charlie's face. But he held his temper. Fighting wasn't the answer. All that would get him was time in the local jail cell, and that was something he preferred to avoid. Couldn't stand even to think about it.

With a shake of his head, he went into the post office.

A plump woman with a round face and cheery expression stood behind a long counter. She greeted him, then asked, "How can I help you?"

"Just need to mail this letter."

"Of course." She held out a hand to take it from him. After glancing at it, her eyes widened. "Well, I'll be. It's been years since Mrs. Grace wrote to her mother."

Julia's mother? For some reason, he'd thought her mother deceased, like his own parents. He'd believed Julia was all alone in the world.

As if echoing his thoughts, the post mistress added, "I thought she must be dead." She looked up. "They wrote each other often when Mrs. Grace first came to Wyoming to live with that husband of hers. My, my. What a handsome couple they made. Angus Grace was a fine-looking man. There was more than one disappointed miss in Pine Creek when he went and married a gal from Idaho. But he hardly ever brought his wife into town, so I can't say I knew Mrs. Grace well. Got used to seeing these letters, though. She wrote to her mother as regular as clockwork, she did. Then all of a sudden, maybe five years back, Angus stopped bringing any more letters into town to mail and right soon the letters from Idaho stopped coming too. I thought it real peculiar at the time, but it was none of my business, of course, so I couldn't very well ask."

Hugh had begun to wonder if the post mistress would pause to draw breath. If a person wanted to keep a secret, it was obvious they shouldn't share it with her.

"Are you working for Mrs. Grace?"

He nodded.

"You tell her I said hello. Will you do that for me? Marjorie O'Donnell's my name."

"I'll do it, ma'am." He touched his hat brim. "Good day."

Although Hugh was glad to escape the talkative post mistress, her comments stayed with him on the ride back to Sage-hen. The more he pondered them, the more they seemed to provide him with new glimpses into Julia's history—and yet much about her remained a mystery to him.

They were alike in that, not wanting to talk about their pasts. He knew his reasons. What were hers?

Twenty

On Wednesday morning, Julia and Hugh were on the trail soon after the sun rose over the mountains, driving the herd of cows and calves south. They would follow the river until it turned west. There, they would turn the cattle east, dropping down onto the plains where they would follow the rails to the Double T Ranch.

In past years, with two or three cowboys riding along with Angus, the drive had been accomplished in two days. Julia hoped they could accomplish it in the same amount of time. Bandit was a good herding dog and could be trusted to keep a lookout for cows who tried to double back. And Hugh, while not accomplished with a rope, rode well, and his gelding could turn quick.

Julia had chosen to sell off just over half her mature cows. It was a gamble but one she was forced to take. And if Mr. Trent at the Double T gave her the price she expected—he'd always been fair—she would be all right. She could pay her taxes, her debt at the mercantile, and Hugh Brennan's wages for a month's work, plus have enough left over to see her through another year. As long as she didn't lose any cattle over the winter to weather or predators and as long as she got a good crop of healthy calves next year, she would be all right.

Why wasn't she encouraged by that belief? Why was her soul still so troubled?

They were close to two hours into the drive when Hugh trotted his horse over to Julia's side. "Looks like we might get some rain." He motioned with his head toward a darkening western horizon.

Rain? It had been clear and sunny for better than three weeks. If it rained now, it would be a miserable few days on the trail.

"Let's try to bunch them up a bit and keep moving. If we get thunder and lightning with that storm, I think we'd be better off down on the plains than where we are now."

With a nod, Hugh fell out to the left. Julia went to the right, both of them shouting, "Ho, there. Ho." Bandit added his barks for good measure and darted at the heels of any stragglers. The cattle bellowed their complaints but complied with the pressure on the flanks of the herd, moving into a closer formation while quickening their pace too.

The sun was close to straight up by the time Julia decided to let the cows and horses stop to rest and graze. The storm that threatened earlier in the morning had rolled north. Now the temperature was climbing. The day was going to end up a scorcher.

Julia and Hugh found a place in some shade to sit. They ate their lunch in silence, and Julia found herself missing the sound of Hugh's voice. They hadn't spoken much to each other since Sunday by the river. She'd been the one to end that conversation, and her action seemed to have put up a wall between them. But she supposed it was better that way. Her feelings for Hugh confused her, and she didn't like being confused.

As if he'd read her thoughts and wanted to change her mind, Hugh said, "The dime novels I've read about the West make a cattle drive seem more exciting than it really is." He washed down the last bite of sandwich with a long draw on the canteen.

"Dime novels? You don't strike me as the type to read those kinds of books." Unable to resist, she added, "The nursery-rhyme type, but not dime novels."

He laughed.

Julia's confusion vanished. Her spirits lifted as a crack appeared in that wall she'd erected.

"I like to read most anything," he said, not seeming to notice her lightened mood. "Biographies are my favorite. But sometimes a man has to settle for whatever's available."

A sixth sense told her he meant something more than lack of funds or access to other literature. *What, Hugh? Tell me what you mean.*

He couldn't read her mind, and he didn't tell

her what he meant. Instead, he asked questions of his own. "What about you, Julia? What do you like to read?"

She looked away, staring into the distance. "My husband believed books were a waste of money and reading a waste of time." The memory made her want to rebuild the wall, made her want to draw inside herself and stay there.

Would the day ever come when she could speak of her dead husband and not feel that twinge of pain, not want to withdraw from the world? God willing, she hoped so.

Hugh was beginning to hate Angus Grace, the dead man who'd left behind a legacy of pain in his widow's eyes. The man who'd kept his wife away from town. The man who hadn't wanted her to read books. She might not have spent years behind bars, as Hugh had, but he suspected she'd been imprisoned all the same. And an innocent prisoner to boot. He knew something about that particular agony.

Abruptly, Julia stood, her hands brushing her riding skirt. "We'd best go. We need to cover a good piece before sunset."

He was sorry the respite was over. There was more he would have liked to ask.

A short while later, the cattle were on the move again. Dust rose in a cloud above the trail. Even though Hugh and Julia rode at the sides of the herd, it was impossible not to be covered in a layer of dirt. He tasted grit on his tongue and felt it in his eyes. He found himself wishing the storm had caught up with them after all. Could a good drenching be any worse than choking on dust? And if it was this bad with a small herd, what must the large cattle drives of twenty and thirty years ago—with a hundred times more cattle and lasting for 2,500 miles—have been like? He shuddered to think.

"Ho, there. Ho!"

Through the dust cloud, he saw Julia turn her horse out and bring back a couple of strays. She was a strong, independent, determined woman. He suspected she'd had plenty of heartache, but she hadn't let it defeat her. She didn't need his help beyond this drive.

But if he could help her . . . if there was a chance that she might ever want—

No. He couldn't and she wouldn't. Better to let it end there.

They stopped at dusk at the mouth of a narrow draw. Dinner was beans warmed over a fire. After they were done, Julia slipped away to the creek that ran nearby and did her best to wash away the dirt of the trail from her face and hair. She would have liked to bathe all over, but the water was too cold for that. A bath would have to wait until they were home again. After toweling dry her hair, she wove it into a damp braid before returning to the campfire. Hugh sat with his side toward the flames, reading his Bible in the flickering light.

"My mother always said I'd ruin my eyes, reading in such poor light."

He closed the cover of the book and looked in her direction. "Mine used to say the same."

"I miss her," she whispered, not meaning to say it aloud, not meaning for him to hear.

"She's still in Idaho." He shrugged. "The envelope. Remember? The post mistress told me who the letter was for."

"Of course she did."

"Was it a secret?"

She shook her head. "No. It's just . . . it's just that my mother hasn't written to me in a long while. We had a . . . a falling out."

"I'm sorry, Julia. I know how that hurts."

His soft response soothed something inside of her. She believed him. The tenderness in his gaze almost overwhelmed her. She wanted . . . something. Something she shouldn't want.

Hugh cleared his throat. "Shall I take the first watch?"

Good heavens! She'd forgotten the cattle, forgotten there was a need to keep watch.

He got to his feet. "I'll wake you in a few hours. Better get some sleep."

Julia watched as he strode to his horse and

swung into the saddle. It was a moonless night, and Hugh didn't have to ride his gelding far to disappear from view. When she could no longer hear the rocks crunching beneath the horse's hooves, she lay on her bedroll, pulled the blanket to her chin, and rolled onto her side, her back to the fire. Before she was settled, Bandit joined her, turning in a slow circle, as if making a nest, then laying down with a grunt.

"You worked hard today." She reached out to stroke his head. "You're a good boy."

The dog responded by closing his eyes.

Julia did the same, and immediately she pictured Hugh as he'd been a short while before, reading his Bible in the firelight. A sense of security, of rightness, perhaps even of hope stole into her heart, and in no time at all, she was fast asleep.

The fire had burned low by the time Hugh returned to camp. A look at his watch by the failing light showed he'd been with the herd for close to five hours. He wished he could let Julia sleep until first light, but he needed a few hours of shut-eye himself.

"What time is it?" she asked groggily after he gently shook her shoulder.

"Almost three." He straightened and moved a few steps away.

She groaned as she sat up. "You should have

woke me before this." In the pale light of the remaining fire, he saw her stretch her arms above her head.

"It's a quiet night. Nothing's stirring."

"Good." She stood and stretched again.

A longing hit Hugh, so strong it almost paralyzed him. He'd wanted to help her before. He'd wanted to protect her before. He'd even wanted to embrace her and kiss her before. But this feeling was different. Now he wanted . . . more. He wanted to promise her the sun and the moon and the stars. He wanted to make her laugh. He wanted to make her dance for joy. It took his breath away, the wanting, and he was thankful for the darkness so that she wouldn't see it in his eyes.

She moved away from her bedroll. Although Hugh couldn't see her clearly, he was aware of her movements as she saddled and bridled Teddy, and he heard the creak of leather as she swung into the saddle.

"Better get some rest," she said before riding off.

He lay down, but sleep evaded him. All he could think about was Julia and the yearning he felt for her. It wasn't lust, wasn't merely a man's desire to possess a woman's body. He knew that physical reaction, knew how to control it rather than being controlled by it. No, this was something different, something rare and fine.

His mind wanted to put a name to the emotion, but he wouldn't allow it. He was a former convict. He'd spent years in prison, surrounded by men who'd done unimaginable things to innocent people. Hugh hadn't been guilty of the charges that placed him in that penitentiary, but he'd been changed for the worst by the experience. Did he think he could walk away from his incarceration without being tainted by those years within its walls? Yes, Christ's blood had washed away his sin, but it didn't undo his past, didn't make him a fit man for a woman like Julia Grace. He squeezed his eyes shut, willing away the thoughts, willing away the feelings that he had no right to feel.

She doesn't know who I am. She doesn't know what I am.

He'd had a chance to tell her the truth when they went to the river for Sunday worship, but something had kept him silent. Perhaps it was God Himself.

And it made no difference whether she knew or not. He had nothing to offer any woman, let alone what he would want to give to Julia.

Twenty-one

The rain they'd escaped the previous day started falling before noon. With it came the wind and dropping temperatures.

Julia and Hugh donned slickers, but water still found its way down their necks, making them cold and miserable. Too miserable to stop to eat their noon meal, so they pressed on toward their destination, determined to reach the Double T Ranch before nightfall.

Years ago, Timothy Trent, owner of the Double T, had built a number of holding pens near the railroad tracks that cut through the length of Wyoming. It was there his cattle waited to be shipped to buyers in Cheyenne, and it was there the small herd from Sage-hen would spend this night. Angus and Timothy had worked out an arrangement that benefited them both—Timothy would pay cash for the cattle at fair value, keeping back a little profit for himself, and then ship them to market with his own herd. Julia was thankful the rancher had been willing to continue the practice after her husband's death.

Several times during the afternoon, Hugh dropped back from the herd, as if looking for something. Or waiting for something. But what? It was gray and gloomy. Julia couldn't see even a quarter mile in any direction. When Hugh caught up again with the herd after the third such time, she asked him what he was doing.

He rubbed the back of his neck. "Maybe it sounds strange, but I've got a feeling someone's been following us today."

"Following us?" She twisted in the saddle and looked back into the murkiness. "If someone's there, he'd be wise to make himself known. If you skulk about in these parts, you're likely to get yourself shot."

"Maybe skulking is the point. Whoever it is might not want to be seen or known." Rainwater ran off the brim of Hugh's hat as he tipped his head in her direction. "This isn't the first time I've suspected something amiss. There was that day I thought something was bothering the cows. Maybe it was the same person who cut the fence."

Maybe it was the same person who encouraged the land board to raise the taxes, Julia thought, remembering that Rose believed Charlie had something to do with it. But that stretched the limits of credulity. Didn't it?

"Your brother-in-law's made it clear he wants you to sell to him," Hugh added, as if reading her thoughts. "Remember, he said he's coming to see you again after you're back from the drive."

"I remember."

"Maybe he's looking for a way to force you to

sell. He seems to know you're struggling to keep your head above water."

She didn't like Charlie Prescott. That was true. But that was because he was Angus's half-brother. He was ambitious. He was determined. He was already the wealthiest man in the county. Yet none of that gave her reason to suspect him of trouble-making.

"Julia, I know something about men like Prescott. He'll stop at nothing to get what he wants."

"You don't know him. You've seen him, what? Twice? You're starting to sound like Rose. She doesn't trust him either."

"Then maybe you should pay heed to what your friend is telling you even if you don't want to listen to me."

She looked at Hugh a moment longer, then kicked Teddy in the sides and moved forward.

They arrived at the Double T holding pens just as the rain finally let up. It didn't take long to get the cattle into a couple of the enclosures. Once that was done, Julia and Hugh rode north toward the ranch house.

Victoria Trent, Timothy's wife, was the one who answered Julia's knock. "Gracious sakes alive!" she exclaimed. "Julia Grace, is that you? You look half drowned."

"At least half."

Victoria grinned. "Come in. Come in." Her gaze flicked to Hugh. "The both of you. Was Timothy expecting you this week? He didn't say a word to me."

"I think so. Isn't he here?"

"No. He's gone to Denver and won't be back until Saturday or Sunday. It must have slipped his mind that you'd be bringing the cattle this week."

Saturday or Sunday? She couldn't wait that long before she returned to Sage-hen. She was already asking too much of Peter. But she needed to return home with the money from the sale.

"Don't you worry," Victoria said. "I can buy your cattle as easy as Timothy does."

"I'm sorry to take you by surprise."

"Not a bother. Now we'd better get the two of you into some warm, dry clothes. I reckon everything in your rolls is as wet as you are."

Embarrassed, Julia lowered her gaze and saw a puddle was forming around her feet. "I'm afraid we're making a mess."

"Don't give it a thought. You think worse things haven't been tracked across the floors of this house? Come on. You too, mister."

She felt another stab of embarrassment. "This is Hugh Brennan. He helped me bring down the herd."

"How do, Mr. Brennan."

200

"Ma'am."

"Just the two of you?" Victoria's eyes returned to Julia.

"Yes." She glanced over her shoulder toward the porch where Bandit sat, waiting for her next command. "And my dog."

"I'll see that he gets something to eat in a bit. For now, you both come with me." Victoria turned and motioned with her hand for them to follow.

In only a few minutes, Julia found herself alone in a bedroom with towels and some borrowed clothes. She didn't waste time getting into them. As the lady of the house was a larger woman, the undergarments were loose on Julia and the dress too long, but she didn't care. She was thankful to be out of her wet things. She was even more thankful when she returned to the main room in the house to find a fire had been started in the fireplace. Hugh was already standing near it.

"There's stew heating up on the stove," Victoria said when she saw Julia. "It won't be long. We'll get you two warmed up, inside and out."

"I didn't expect to put you to all this trouble, Mrs. Trent. We should—"

Victoria laughed. "Gracious sakes alive. You don't know how much I get to hankering for female company. I'm glad to have you here. Glad we can get better acquainted. We barely got introduced last year before you were headed back to that place of yours."

"I know. I'm sorry."

"You'd best stop apologizing right now." She pointed to a chair near the fireplace. "Sit yourself down."

Julia nodded and sank obediently onto the indicated chair.

"You too, Mr. Brennan."

"I'd better take care of the horses first and make sure Bandit's okay," he said.

"No need." Victoria sat on the sofa. "While you were changing, I had one of the boys take your horses and the dog to the barn. They've got plenty of food and water."

"That was good of you, ma'am."

"Not at all. Like I said, I'm delighted to have some female company." Victoria looked at Julia again. "Now tell me, how are you managing on your own? I thought about you more than once over the winter, wondering how you were getting along. This isn't an easy country for a woman who's lost her husband."

Julia gave a slight shrug. "I've managed well enough." True words, if one didn't count the higher taxes on her land.

"Last year when we met, I told Timothy that you were such a slight thing, I was afraid a good wind would just pick you up and blow you away. You looked so pale in your widow's weeds." The older woman's tender look was almost as warming as the fire. "But look at you now. I can see you are much recovered from losing Mr. Grace."

"Yes," Julia answered softly. But she didn't think she and Victoria meant the same thing.

Hugh watched Julia and wondered at the different expressions that played across her face. She wasn't as good as Hugh at hiding her emotions, but that didn't mean she was always easy to read either. His mum used to say, *"There are deep secrets in a woman's heart, Hugh. Remember that when you come of age. T'will serve you well if you're having that understanding."* She'd most surely meant a woman like Julia.

"Well, at least you've got a strong man to help you now, Mrs. Grace. That takes away some of the worry, I'm sure." To Hugh she said, "Have you been working at Sage-hen long, Mr. Brennan? You weren't with Julia last year."

"No. I haven't been there long."

"I see my son's clothes fit you about as good as mine fit Mrs. Grace."

Hugh glanced down at the trousers he wore. They were comfortable in the waist and hips, but the hem of the pant legs hit him in mid-shin. He hadn't given the fit any thought until she pointed it out. This wasn't the first time he'd worn clothes not meant for someone of his height. When a man had little, he learned to make do with what little he had.

Not that I speak in respect of want, Paul wrote in the Bible, *for I have learned, in whatsoever state I am, therewith to be content.* Good advice for a man like him.

"Well, no matter," Victoria continued. "Your own things'll be dry by morning."

"Are you sure we aren't too much trouble?" Julia asked again. "We'd planned to sleep on the trail, same as we did last night."

Victoria frowned at her. "Thought we'd settled that. I won't have you starting back all wet and cold. Not when I've got extra rooms and beds for you to sleep in."

Hugh had only met this rancher's wife a half an hour ago, but he would wager Julia was no match for her. To argue was futile.

"Now, you'd best excuse me while I check on that stew. It ought to be ready." Victoria rose and hurried out of the main parlor, through the dining room, and disappeared into what Hugh supposed was the kitchen.

"I didn't expect that we'd be asked to stay," Julia said softly, drawing his gaze back to her.

"She's being kind, the same way you are to others. Same way you've been to me."

Julia's cheeks turned pink, and he understood that she wasn't anymore used to compliments than he was.

I'd like to change that. There they were again, those same feelings he'd determined not to allow

204

himself to feel for her. Desire. Affection. A need to be close to her. A hunger to be with her every minute of every day.

"Come along, you two," Victoria called from the next room. "Come and eat while it's good and hot."

Hugh stepped toward Julia's chair and offered his hand. She hesitated a moment before placing her fingers against his palm. He closed his hand around hers, then with a gentle pull, he helped her rise.

Her eyes still averted, she said, "Thank you."

"You're welcome." Reluctantly, he released her hand.

She stepped in front of him and led the way into the dining room.

It was a bigger room than he'd expected. The table would easily sit a party of sixteen or even twenty. Either the Trents had—or once planned to have—a large family or they regularly fed all the employees on their ranch at this table.

Victoria had placed bowls of stew in front of two chairs at the far end of the table, opposite each other. "Come and have a seat. There's stew and bread and butter. You've got your choice of milk or coffee to drink. Both if you want 'em. And I made a cherry cobbler today with a mighty fine crust, if I do say so myself." She pulled out the chair at the end of the table and sat down.

Hugh and Julia took their appointed places.

"Care to bless the food, Mr. Brennan?" Victoria asked before bowing her head.

A month or two ago, Hugh would have felt self-conscious, praying in front of strangers. But he'd grown more comfortable after so many meals—and blessings—with Julia, so he obliged without hesitation. Afterward, while he and Julia ate, their hostess carried on an easy conversation, occasionally asking questions. But she seemed satisfied with a nod or a brief word or two for answers.

Hugh had just taken his last bite of cherry cobbler—the woman was right; it had a mighty fine crust—when a cowboy appeared in the kitchen doorway. "Miz Trent."

"Yes, Whitey?"

"Sorry to bother you, ma'am, but there's been some trouble at the stock pens."

Hugh saw Julia tense.

"What sort of trouble?"

"Somebody opened the gates and let out the cows."

"Good heavens!"

The cowboy shook his head as he looked at Julia. "Not to worry, Miz Grace. Didn't any get far. But we didn't see who did it or where he went. We'll try to pick up his trail in the mornin', though I don't reckon we'll find him after all this rain."

Hugh scooted his chair back from the table and

stood. "I'll keep watch down at the pens for the night," he said to Julia. Looking at Victoria, he added, "Thanks for the meal, Mrs. Trent. It was good."

"You're more than welcome, Mr. Brennan. But you needn't go. Our boys'll make sure nothing more goes amiss."

"All the same, I think I'd better go down there."

Victoria nodded. "Whitey, show Mr. Brennan to the barn so he can saddle his horse."

At the end of a rainy day, sunset splashed a glorious display of pinks and purples upon the rain clouds' underbellies as Peter arrived home from Sage-hen. He took a moment to enjoy the colorful sky, then put up his horse and headed into the house. All was quiet within, the children having been sent to bed. A light beneath the three oldest girls' bedroom door told him at least one of them was still awake. He heard one of them giggle as he stepped close to the door.

"I think he has beautiful eyes." Abigail's voice.

"They're just eyes." This from Bathshua. "No prettier than Pa's or Uncle Roland's."

Abigail again. "How can you say that? Mark's eyes are the bluest blue I've ever seen. And they spark when he laughs."

Mark? Mark Kittson? He remembered Julia saying something about Abigail getting engaged soon and hadn't he noticed the Kittson boy coming round their place all spring. He hadn't wanted to believe it, but it looked like Julia could be right.

He shook his head as he moved down the hall toward his own bedroom. A light still burned there too. His wife never turned out the lamp until he was in bed beside her.

Rose was seated in a wingback chair, knitting needles clicking away. "You're home," she said as he closed the door behind him. "It's late."

"Yeah, it took a little longer than I expected."

"Everything okay at Julia's?"

"Yep."

"Tomorrow you take one of the girls with you. You'll get done in half the time. You're working too hard as it is."

"There's nothing wrong with me, Rosie."

"Those stitches in your head say different."

He walked over to where she sat and bent over to kiss the top of her head. "Quit worrying about me. I'm fine."

Rose sighed her agreement before setting aside the needles and yarn. "I think the girls are asleep."

"Not all of them. I heard Abigail and Bathshua talking when I came in." He went to the opposite side of the room, shrugging out of his suspenders and slipping off his shirt. "Julia seems to think Abigail and Mark Kittson have formed an attachment for each other. I told her I didn't think so but—"

"Peter Collins, are you telling me you only just noticed?" His wife laughed. "Why that boy goes positively tongue-tied every time Abigail gets within ten yards of him. He's been that way for the past six months or more."

"But you don't think it's serious, do you?" He dropped his nightshirt over his head.

Rose's arms went around his waist from behind, and she gave him a squeeze. Then he turned and gathered her close, glad she'd left her chair and come to stand with him. Glory, but he loved this woman. God had been good to bring them together. "Abigail's too young," he whispered into her hair.

"I was in love with you at that age."

"I know but it . . . it's different somehow."

Rose laughed again. "It's different because she's your daughter." She raised up on tiptoe and kissed him on the mouth. "You'd better get used to it, my love. You have ten daughters and we're going to have boys coming courting for the next eighteen or twenty years."

He groaned—half in jest, half in earnest—then drew her with him to the bed.

"You mustn't worry, Mrs. Grace," Victoria said. "The boys'll protect the cattle. Besides, they're Trent cattle now."

Julia pushed her chair away from the table, intending to rise. "They're my cattle until we

209

complete the transaction and you pay me for them. I should go with Hugh."

Victoria stopped her by laying a hand on her arm. "Dear girl, do you mind a word of advice?"

Julia shook her head.

"A man likes to be a man. He likes to take care of his woman. Let your Mr. Brennan look out for the cows. It's one way of him sayin' he cares for you."

"My Mr. . . . cares for . . . You're mistaken, Mrs. Trent. Hugh Brennan works for me. That's all. We are nothing more than employer and employee."

The older woman's eyes were skeptical as she studied Julia. After a lengthy silence, she said, "Maybe on your part—if you insist, though I doubt it—but you're wrong about his feelings for you. Saw it as clear as day."

Julia looked toward the kitchen doorway where Hugh had disappeared from view a short time before. She wanted to tell Victoria that she was the one who was wrong, but then she remembered the way he looked at her sometimes and the tone of his voice when he spoke to her.

Could it be true?

Julia turned toward Victoria. "I don't want him to care. I have no intention of ever marrying again."

"No? Well, let me tell you this. It's good for a woman to love her husband while he's livin', but learnin' to love again after he's gone doesn't take away from that. You don't run out of the capacity to love, you know. There's always more love available."

Love? Love for Angus? No, that wasn't the reason she would never marry again. She hadn't ever had a chance to learn to love her husband. She'd wanted to. She'd tried to. She'd married him believing—as only a young and foolish and romantic girl could—that love would grow between them. But he hadn't cared if she loved him or not.

"You would have no way of knowing this," Victoria continued, "but Mr. Trent wasn't my first husband. I was married before. Michael was his name, and oh my, I did love that man with everything in me. But he was killed in an accident and left me a widow with a small son to raise. I didn't know how I was going to manage. And then I met Timothy Trent. His love healed my heart, and we built a good life together, we and our sons."

"You're very blessed," Julia said, her throat tight.

"Don't I know it. And all I'm sayin' is, don't close yourself off from love when it comes knockin' at your door. You never know what the good Lord might have in store for you if you just say yes to it."

Julia rubbed her forehead with the fingers of her right hand, trying to massage away the pressure that was starting to build. "I hope you won't think me rude, Mrs. Trent, but I believe I'd like to retire."

"Not rude at all. If I'd spent two days trailin' a bunch of cows, my head would be achin' too. Not to mention my backside." She released a soft laugh. "You go on. A good night's sleep'll make all the difference. You'll see things clearer in the morning."

Julia hoped her hostess was right. But first she had to *fall* asleep, and she wasn't sure when that would happen. Not with thoughts of Hugh Brennan filling her head.

Oh please, God. Mrs. Trent has to be wrong. I don't want him to care for me. Not that way.

Twenty-two

Hugh returned to the ranch house just before dawn. Three of the Trent cowboys had stayed behind to continue the watch, although no one thought the rustler—if stealing the cattle had been the troublemaker's intent—would return.

Hugh went into the bedroom that Mrs. Trent had shown him to the previous evening and barely got out of the borrowed clothes before he fell onto the bed and into an exhausted sleep. When he awakened a few hours later, he found his own clothes folded on a chair just inside the doorway. He poured water into the bowl on the dresser and washed up, then dressed and went in search of Julia. He found her where he'd left her the night before, in the dining room, holding a cup of coffee with both hands as she took a sip.

"Morning," he said.

The look she gave him seemed strained. "Good morning."

"Sorry I slept so long."

She motioned toward the sideboard. "Breakfast is there, though it's likely a bit cold."

"Thanks." He took a plate and filled it with biscuits and gravy and fried sausage. Then he sat on the chair.

"Mrs. Trent told me there was no more trouble in the night," Julia said.

"No. No more. It was quiet."

"She also said they haven't had trouble with cattle thieves in many years, so this attempt was unexpected."

He took a bite of his breakfast while he waited for Julia to continue.

"I suppose we're lucky all the rustler had time to do was open the gates."

Hugh wanted to bring up Charlie Prescott again, but he doubted she would listen to him. Still, his gut told him he was right. Whatever the man's motives, her brother-in-law was behind this attempt to steal her cattle. And Hugh was certain Charlie Prescott wouldn't stop at stealing cattle or cutting barbed wire if those things didn't get him what he wanted. He was capable of much worse. What would he try after Hugh was gone?

The question sent a chill through him.

Julia leaned down from the saddle and shook Victoria Trent's outstretched hand. "Thanks again for your hospitality."

"Not at all. The least we can do for a neighbor." Victoria took a step backward. "You take care of yourself, Mrs. Grace."

"Thanks."

"And you remember what I told you last night." Julia nodded. "I will."

Victoria turned toward Hugh. "It was good to meet you, Mr. Brennan."

"You too, ma'am."

"You keep an eye out for Mrs. Grace. You hear?"

"I will." His gaze flicked toward Julia, then back again.

Julia's pulse quickened. She didn't want Hugh keeping an eye out for her. His work was almost over. The herd had been delivered. She had the money from the sale. When they got back to Sage-hen, she could pay him and send him on his way. That was for the best. For her. For him.

Wasn't it?

The storm that had accompanied them to the Double T had moved on, leaving behind blue skies, a refreshed green to the landscape, and cooler temperatures. Julia decided to push hard toward home, resting only when the horses and Bandit grew tired. Without the cattle to slow them down, they could make the journey in one day, despite leaving later in the morning than desired. Hugh seemed no more inclined to start or carry on a conversation than Julia, for which she was thankful. Except the silence gave her more time to think, more time to worry, more time to wonder. About Sage-hen. About the coming year. About higher taxes. About rustlers. About Charlie.

About Hugh.

No, not about Hugh. She wouldn't think or worry or wonder about Hugh. She wouldn't. She mustn't.

Both physically and mentally weary, she was never more glad to ride into the barnyard at Sage-hen than she was that Friday evening. Dusk had washed the house and outbuildings in tones of gray. Her two wagon horses had been moved from one paddock to another, just one evidence that Peter had been over to tend the livestock in her absence. Cattle grazed on the green spring grass within sight of the barnyard.

"I'll see to the horses," Hugh said as they dismounted.

"Thanks." She removed the saddlebags that held the precious payment for the cattle and passed Teddy's reins to Hugh. Then she headed for the house, Bandit leading the way. Once in her bedroom, she took the money box from its hiding place and put the cash she'd received from Victoria Trent in it. Come Monday, bright and early, she would go into Pine Creek. She would visit the county courthouse to pay her taxes. She would pay her bill at the mercantile, and she would deposit whatever money was left in the bank.

As she closed and locked the box, she wondered if Hugh would want to be paid for his work tonight or in the morning. And would he leave right away or would he stay a few days longer to rest his horse as she'd suggested? Loneliness rolled over her with a sudden fierceness, the thought of being at Sage-hen without Hugh almost unbearable. Tears pricked her eyes. She blinked them back, at the same time swallowing a lump that rose in her throat.

"I'm tired and hungry," she said aloud. "Once I've eaten and had a good night's sleep, I won't feel this way."

She liked being alone. She truly, truly did.

After building a fire in the stove, she scrambled most of the eggs Peter had collected while they were away. More than half went to Bandit along with some leftover strips of dried venison. While the dog scarfed down his dinner, Julia went onto the porch. Evening had arrived in earnest, and since the moon had yet to rise, the barn had become a slightly darker shadow amid many shadows.

"Hugh?" she called.

He appeared a short while later with a lantern in hand.

"Are you hungry? I scrambled some eggs."

"Thanks. I wouldn't object to eating something." He walked toward her.

He won't be here much longer. He won't eat at my table many more times.

Julia turned on her heel, as if running from the thought.

She's running from me.

Hugh saw it and felt it. Was he surprised? No. Not at all. What surprised him was that she'd ever let him get close to her—physically or emotionally—at all. His work was done. It was time for him to leave. He stepped onto the porch and put the lantern down near the doorway, then he moved inside.

Julia was in the kitchen, setting a large plate of eggs on the table. Without looking at him, she said, "Not much of a supper. You must be sick and tired of scrambled eggs by now."

"I've eaten worse things." He said it lightly, as if it were a joke. It wasn't. He'd eaten much worse. He'd gone without too. Been so hungry he thought—

She straightened, her eyes now meeting his.

Questions hovered in their blue depths. Questions he wasn't willing to answer.

They sat at the table and, after a quick blessing, ate their supper. It wasn't until Hugh pushed back his empty plate that Julia spoke again.

"I should give you your pay."

"Tomorrow is soon enough."

"When do you plan to leave?" she asked softly. "Didn't you say Monday?"

"Yeah, Monday. Unless you need me to stay longer." Hope rose in his chest, warring with commonsense as he awaited her answer.

She shook her head. "I've kept you from your journey long enough. I want . . . I want you to know how much I've appreciated all you've done for me. And for helping Peter too when he needed it."

"I'm glad I could do it." He hesitated a moment, then added, "I wish there was more I could do to help you."

"But there isn't. I'm used to managing on my own, and you've repaired just about everything that needed fixing."

"What about Charlie Prescott?"

She drew a deep breath and let it out on a sigh. "I can handle him. He's a bother. Nothing more. I have no need to sell the ranch. My taxes will be paid come Monday and so will my bill at the mercantile."

"Taxes?"

218

"Yes. They're due soon, and they're . . . they're higher than a year ago."

I'd like to take away your worries, Julia. I'd like to pay those taxes for you. I'd like to protect you from men like Charlie Prescott. I'd like you to know what it is to be loved and cherished, and maybe you'd learn to love me in return.

Her face paled. Her eyes rounded.

If I told you the sort of man I used to be, could you ever feel for me the same way Rose feels for Peter? The way I feel for you now. Is there a chance—

She stood. "I'll get your pay." She hurried off to her bedroom.

He had his answer. She couldn't be more clear about it if she said it aloud.

Twenty-three

Hugh sat up, panic choking his air supply. The details of the nightmare—barred doors, small rooms, unrelieved darkness, dangerous men— were already receding, but the fear the dream had stirred inside him was not so easily forgotten.

He lowered his feet off the side of the bed and rested his head in his hands. For several weeks—almost his entire time at Sage-hen—his sleep had been undisturbed by nightmares. Strange, how quickly he'd become accustomed to their absence. So much so that he'd believed they were gone for good.

It wasn't just this place, although he was sure that was part of it. Hard work made a man sleep hard too. No, it was Julia who had helped drive away the bad dreams. Knowing her, seeing her faith, learning to care for her—it had all changed him.

But now it was time for him to leave, and the nightmares had returned.

He remained where he was until his pulse returned to normal. Then he arose, lit the lantern, and got dressed. His Bible lay open on the small table, inviting him to find comfort in its pages, but he felt too restless to sit still and read. He needed to move around.

Taking the lantern with him, he left his sleeping quarters. His first stop was to check on the cat and her kittens. After another attempt to relocate her litter, the feline seemed ready to keep her babies where Julia wanted them to stay. Funny, he would miss looking in on them every day. Their eyes were open now, just, but they still weren't very mobile. He didn't know much about cats, but Julia had said they would start to walk in another week. He wouldn't have minded seeing that.

There were plenty of things he wouldn't have minded seeing, given enough time on this ranch. Perhaps most of all, he would have liked to see what became of the hope growing inside of him. Hope for the man he was becoming. Hope that he could have a life he hadn't dared want before. Hope that Julia could learn to love him as he loved her.

He loved her. He loved her more than he'd known it was possible to love.

He turned away from the stall and walked toward the open door of the barn. The night air drifting through was cool, still fresh from the rainstorm of two days before. Silence swathed the barnyard. All nature slept beneath a full moon.

His gaze moved toward the house, and he was surprised to see a light burning from within. Then he saw a shadow move across a window. Julia was awake too.

A sense of foreboding swamped him. The hairs on the back of his neck raised, like the hackles on a dog. That same feeling of danger he'd felt on the trail returned. That sense someone was following or watching, that trouble was coming. He'd been right then that they were being followed. What if—

Hugh set down the lantern and bolted across the yard. He knocked once, hard, and shouted Julia's name. Then he lifted the latch and pushed open the door.

She was seated on a chair in the parlor, a wooden box on her lap. But when the door slammed against the wall, she jumped to her feet.

The box fell to the floor, spilling its contents. Bandit sounded an alarm.

"Are you all right?" Hugh swept the room with his gaze, certain he would find Charlie Prescott or one of his minions somewhere, threatening Julia, lurking in the shadows.

"All right?" Julia pressed her right hand against her collarbone, as if to still her heart. "Of course I'm all right. Bandit, sit. Quiet."

The spaniel obeyed but kept a disapproving eye on Hugh.

He looked around the room a second time. "I saw you were up. It's the middle of the night and I . . . I thought—"

"I'm perfectly all right, Hugh. I just couldn't sleep. And you?"

I'm an idiot. "Couldn't sleep." He looked at her again.

Her hair hung soft and free about the shoulders of her white nightgown. She looked as he imagined an angel would look, pure and sweet and—

She dropped to her knees and began to retrieve the spilled items.

"Let me." He reached for the ring that had rolled across the floor and been stopped by the toe of his boot. As he straightened, he looked at it. His eyes widened. He hadn't worked for his father without learning to spot rare gems and expensive jewelry. Not what he expected to find in this simple log house. "You should take better care of this." He handed it to her. "That's worth more than the cattle you sold to the Trents."

"What?" She looked at the ring, then back at Hugh. "It is? I've never thought it worth much of anything. It's rather ugly, don't you think? What makes you think it's valuable?"

There it was. Another opportunity to tell her who he'd been, what he'd been, where he'd been. But he didn't take it. Why tell her now when he would be gone in a couple more days? "My father knew something about the value of jewelry, and he taught me how to judge stones as a boy." The truth. Just not the whole truth.

"You must be mistaken. The ring belonged . . . it belonged to my husband's mother, and he never said it was valuable."

Hugh shrugged, uncomfortable with where this discussion might take them. "Maybe he didn't know."

"Maybe." She dropped the ring in the box with the other items and closed the lid. "I'm sorry my wakefulness alarmed you. Thank you for your concern."

The urge to take her in his arms, to crush her against him, to kiss her mouth and taste her sweetness rushed over him. If he'd scared her by barging into the parlor, he could just imagine the terror she would feel if he were to act on his desires.

I love you, Julia.

She shook her head as if she'd heard his thoughts. "Good night, Hugh."

With a nod, he took several steps backward and departed, closing the door as he went.

The open door had let in the cool night air, but Julia felt strangely warm as she sank onto the chair once again. She'd seen something in Hugh's eyes, something both strange and familiar, something both frightening and exhilarating. She was relieved he was gone, and yet she felt his absence, like a gaping hole. How much worse that hole would be when Hugh rode away from Sage-hen for the last time.

Drawing a deep breath, she opened the lid of the box one more time. She picked up the ring. Valuable? But it wasn't even pretty. Could he be right? Was it worth more than she'd been paid for her cattle? If that were true—

But it couldn't be true. Angus had told her it was merely cut glass. If it was valuable, he would have taunted her with it, told her he wouldn't let her wear it because she was so unworthy. Then again, he hadn't wanted his half-brother to know about it. Perhaps because it was worth so much?

No, Hugh was wrong about it. And besides, it could make no difference in the middle of the night. Best she go to bed and try to get some sleep.

She put the ring in the box, then she returned the box to its spot in the wardrobe. Bandit went to his favorite place on the rug near the bed and made a few circles before settling into his curled position. Julia gave his head a couple of strokes and got into bed, snuggling down beneath the covers. But when she closed her eyes, she envisioned Hugh and her insides seemed to roll around like a tumbleweed before the wind.

He's leaving soon. Life will return to normal.

Normal was a childhood spent alone in a shack or alone in a room above a saloon. Normal was school children saying awful things about her mother. Normal was a husband who was cold and loveless and sometimes cruel. Normal was the feeling of the back of his hand against her cheek. Normal was the pain of burying a stillborn child, then a second. Normal was living alone on this ranch, sleeping alone in this bed, wondering how she would make it through another summer, another winter.

I don't want normal. I want Hugh.

But she couldn't want him. They couldn't have a future together even if he did care for her. She would never marry again. She could never give ownership of herself to another man to do with as he pleased. And that's what marriage was. Giving oneself away.

Husbands, love your wives, even as Christ also loved the church.

Was it possible for any man to love like that? Perhaps. Peter might love Rose that way. Were there others? Could Hugh Brennan be such a man?

She rolled onto her side and drew her knees toward her chest, trying to drive Hugh's image from her mind, trying not to remember him as they'd sat near the campfire on the cattle drive. Trying not to remember the easy way he sat a horse. Trying not to remember him at the table with his head bowed in prayer or as they ate their meals. Trying not to remember him wielding an ax, making certain she would have ample firewood for the winter. Trying not to remember him holding one of the kittens. Trying not to remember his smiles or his laughter or his tenderness or his concern.

The minutes of the night marched toward dawn while she lay there, sleepless, unsettled, and confused.

Julia was dressed before the sun was full up on Saturday morning. She hurried through her chores, and as soon as possible, she saddled Teddy and rode to her spot by the river, her Bible and journal in the saddlebag.

The water continued to run high in early June, churning, foaming, and tumbling its way south. The sounds of the rushing river—steady and powerful—were soothing to her troubled spirit. While Bandit sniffed among the brush along the bank, Julia settled onto the rocky outcropping. She picked up her Bible, thinking she would read for a while, but instead she lay on her back and closed her eyes. Unlike the previous night when her thoughts had churned and spun and refused to let her be, her mind now seemed empty. She couldn't even form a prayer, although the need to pray was real enough.

But perhaps empty was what she should be. Empty of herself. Empty of her concerns. Empty of anything and everything she put before God.

What do I put before You, Lord?

There was silence in her spirit, and for a moment, she tried to believe the silence meant she didn't make anything an idol, that she put nothing before or above her Maker. But it wasn't true. She sat up and looked around, at the land and trees, at the river and sky. She looked at Sage-hen and knew she sometimes put it first. She'd found her security in this place after the death of her husband, and that's why she was so determined not to lose it. Because if she lost her home, however would she survive?

Isn't God able to provide a way?

An image of her mother came to her, her mother in a fancy nightgown and robe, her face painted, her hair piled high atop her head and decorated with an ostrich feather. Her mother, a woman who'd lived a desperate life, far from God, but who'd also tried to make sure the same thing didn't happen to her daughter. She'd sent Julia to school and to church. She'd kept her away from the worst elements in the mining town.

And then she gave me in marriage to Angus Grace.

That's what came of not listening to the Spirit, of trusting in human wisdom rather than trusting in God. For on the surface, Angus had seemed a good choice for a husband, even to Julia. He'd owned his own ranch. He'd been youthful and handsome. He'd seemed kind and respectable. He'd promised to take care of her.

But his promise had been a lie. He'd been physically cruel and emotionally cold all the years of their marriage. He'd broken her heart and spirit in a hundred different ways, killing her hopes and dreams, nearly destroying her faith.

Fear not, a voice whispered into her heart.

"Fear not," she repeated aloud.

Again she looked at her surroundings, but she seemed to see it with different eyes now. It was land. Beautiful land. Familiar land. But land couldn't make her secure. Nor could solitude. Only God could give her security on this earth. Job said the Lord gave and the Lord took away. She would determine to trust Him to care for her as He cared for the lilies of the field and the birds of the air.

Thou shalt love the Lord thy God with all thy heart, and with all thy soul, and with all thy mind.

"Yes, Lord. I'll love You with all my heart and soul and mind. I'll trust You and not be afraid."

She reached for her journal and pencil and began to write. Where at first she'd felt empty, now she was full to overflowing. There were so many things to say to God on these blank, white pages, and she had to write swiftly before the thoughts took wing.

It was close to noon, the sun baking the hard-packed dirt of the barnyard, when Hugh set the horse's hoof on the ground and straightened. That was the moment a rider came into view. Charlie Prescott. Hugh felt the dislike well up inside him, but years of practice kept it from showing on his face. Moving away from the horse, he wiped his hands on his trousers. Charlie barely gave him a glance as he rode up close to the porch and dismounted.

"Mrs. Grace isn't here," Hugh said in a moderated voice.

Charlie turned, the reins in hand. "Where is she?"

He didn't answer.

"You seem to have made yourself at home, Brennan, but I wouldn't get used to it if I were you. It's past time for you to move on."

Hugh crossed the barnyard until there was little more than a few feet between them. Although it was difficult, he resisted the urge to clench his fists and knock that self-satisfied smirk off Charlie's face.

"It isn't all that difficult to discover the truth about someone if you have a little information to start with. Like a name and where they're from." Charlie's smile held no warmth. "For instance, you. Does Julia know what sort of man she's allowed to work on this sorry little ranch? Because I know who you are and what you've done."

Hugh remained silent, despite the tightening in his gut.

Charlie laughed softly. "It doesn't matter if you answer or not. Because if you don't leave, I will make sure she learns every sordid detail. The sheriff already knows. He'll be watching you, waiting for you to make a mistake."

Hugh clenched his fists at his sides.

"Don't get in my way, Brennan, or I'll make you pay for your interference."

"I'm staying as long as Julia wants me to."

"Do you think she'll be able to hang on here? Not a chance, I promise you." Anger reddened Charlie's face. "My fool brother died without a will or this land would be mine already. He never would have left it to his wife if he'd known he was dying. She knows that's true. I asked her to sell it to me. Offered her a good price too. Now it's too late. She won't be able to pay her taxes. I'll have this place and she'll have nothing."

"She's able to pay them."

The man's eyes narrowed.

"I think it's time you got off her land." Hugh spoke in a soft voice, but Charlie couldn't mistake the threat behind his words.

"You have no—"

"Get on your horse and ride out of here." He took another step toward Charlie. "Now. And don't come around bothering her again."

Charlie's confidence seemed to falter. He went to his horse's side and stepped into the saddle. As he gathered the reins, he said, "You'd better leave, Brennan, before you find yourself in more trouble than you can handle. Before you find yourself back in jail." Then he spun his horse around and cantered away.

Hugh didn't draw a breath until Charlie Prescott was out of sight, his parting words echoing in Hugh's mind: *"Before you find yourself back in jail."* Somehow, Charlie—and the sheriff—had discovered the truth about him. *"Before you find yourself back in jail."* His past would follow him wherever he went. It didn't matter if he kept his nose clean. At the first hint of trouble, he would be thought guilty.

Guilty.

Funny, in a way. He'd gotten away scot-free for things he'd actually done as a boy, then he'd spent a decade in prison for something he hadn't done.

Guilty.

As if it had happened yesterday, Hugh heard the verdict and the slap of the judge's gavel. He saw the faces of the men on the jury, smelled the musty air of the courtroom, and noted the continued absence of the man who could have cleared his name: his father. Sweeney Brennan had abandoned his son to what passed for justice in Chicago. It had taken a long time to forgive his father for that betrayal. Longer still to understand that if Sweeney had come forward there would have been two Brennans in jail rather than just Hugh.

He took a deep breath as he strode toward the barn.

"Before you find yourself back in jail."

Guilty.

"Before you find yourself back in jail."

Guilty.

It was wrong of him to want to love Julia. It was wrong of him to want to stay with her. She didn't know the truth about him. If he left now, Charlie would have no reason to tell her. Besides, Hugh had an obligation to his sisters. It was the need to find them that had brought him west in the first place. He had no right to want to remain in Wyoming, to want to put down roots, to want to make a life for himself, to want a wife and family.

A wife and family. The words drifted through his heart, like a leaf floating to the ground on a soft autumn's day. Marriage to Julia. Children with Julia. Impossible wishes. Impractical hopes. Unfeasible dreams.

Besides, hadn't Paul written that a man who was unmarried was better off to stay that way? He was certain he'd read that in one of the apostle's letters. Yet he'd also read that a man was to love his wife the way Christ loved the church, enough to die for her. Hugh loved Julia that way. Or at least he wanted to love her that way.

"I have nothing to offer her. What kind of man would marry a woman when he owns nothing more than a horse and a Bible?"

Not the kind of man he hoped to become. Not the kind of man Julia deserved.

Why wait until Monday? He had his wages. He had the supplies he would need to make it to Boise City.

It was time he was on his way.

Twenty-four

That morning by the river, Julia filled many pages in her journal with thoughts, prayers, and Bible verses. The words were honest, even brutal. Perhaps more honest than anything she'd written between its covers before, revealing emotions she'd rarely—if ever—allowed herself to acknowledge feeling. And when she was done, when she couldn't write another word, she gathered her belongings, swung into the saddle, and rode Teddy toward the Collins farm, needing the sound counsel of her closest friend.

As if Rose had awaited her arrival, she was standing on the front porch when Julia rode into the barnyard. "I didn't expect to see you so soon," she called to her. "Were you late getting home?"

"Not very." Julia slipped from the saddle and looped Teddy's reins around a post before stepping onto the porch.

"Was it a successful trip?"

"Yes. I'll have enough money to see me through to next spring."

Rose's eyes narrowed slightly. "You don't sound very happy about it."

"Don't I?" She shook her head. "No, I suppose I don't. That's why I'm here, I guess. To talk to you."

"Come inside. I can have tea ready in no time at all."

Julia knew that, for Rose, tea equaled comfort. She nodded. She needed comfort along with her friend's wisdom.

The two women moved inside.

"Where is everyone?" Julia asked into the silence.

"Hope, India, and the baby are sleeping. Peter and the rest of the girls went to call on the Thompsons. Mrs. Thompson's been ailing, so I sent her some cinnamon rolls. She's always liked my rolls."

Julia sat at the table. "Who doesn't?"

"Would you like one?" Standing at the stove, Rose glanced over her shoulder. "I kept some for the family."

"Not right now."

Rose put the kettle on to boil, then joined Julia at the table. "All right. You'd best tell me what has you so troubled."

"Rose, I think—" She drew in a deep breath. "I think I'm falling in love."

"With Mr. Brennan?" her friend asked softly.

Julia nodded.

A smile brightened Rose's face. "But that's a reason for gladness."

"He's leaving. Monday."

"Have you told him how you feel?"

She shook her head.

"Well, for pity sake. Do so. He cares for you a great deal, Julia. It's plain as the nose on your face."

Victoria Trent had told her almost the exact same thing. Were Hugh's feelings evident to everyone but her? Or perhaps they *were* evident to her. She pictured him looking at her. Many different times. Many different ways. Something softened inside her heart.

"Do you truly think he would stay if he knew?"

Rose leaned closer. "You'll never know unless

you tell him. If you told him and he left anyway, would you feel any worse than if you keep silent?"

"I guess not."

The kettle began to whistle, and Rose went to see to their tea.

Julia had never told a man she loved him. If she said those words to Hugh and he left her anyway, she feared it might shatter her heart into a thousand pieces. And if he didn't leave, if he wanted to marry her, was she ready to let him become part of every aspect of her life? Was she willing to let go of the freedom she'd gained when Angus died?

"Julia."

She looked at her friend who was facing her again, tea cups in hand.

"Love is a risk. But it's a risk worth taking."

Hugh loped his gelding along the road north of Pine Creek, trying to ignore the desire in his heart that told him to turn around and go back. There were a hundred reasons why it was better that he leave. Better for Julia. Better for him.

He'd left a note for her, expressing his gratitude, but the farther he got from the ranch the more it felt like cowardice to not talk to her face-to-face, to leave without telling her the whole truth and seeing if there might be a chance for him, for them.

What was he supposed to do? How could he possibly know God's will in this regard?

Julia hadn't brought Teddy to a stop before she noticed two things: Hugh's horse wasn't in the paddock or corral and the front door of the house was wide open. A split second later, Bandit faced the porch and growled, his back hunched, his head lowered.

"Quiet, boy." She slipped the rifle from its sheath before easing down from the saddle.

She took a couple of steps, then stopped, unsure what to do next. If an intruder was inside, was it better to wait where she was or to go in and confront him? Should she give some indication of her return or proceed as quietly as possible?

If Hugh was with her, he would know what to do. But he wasn't with her. Not at this moment. Perhaps never again after Monday.

She drew a deep breath. She couldn't think about that now. "You in the house," she called. "Come outside. With your hands up."

No one came out. Bandit looked at Julia.

"Is someone in there, boy?"

The dog took her question as a command, moving forward, sniffing and listening as he went. Julia waited, heart in throat, until he'd disappeared through the open doorway. When nothing happened, when Bandit gave no cry of alarm, she walked toward the house, rifle at ready. A quick glance upon entering the parlor revealed nothing out of place, there or in the kitchen.

"Hello?"

No answer. No unusual sounds.

I'm being silly. She released a deep breath and lowered the rifle.

Bandit reappeared in her bedroom doorway.

"I must have left the door unlatched and it blew open."

The dog gave a little whine, then turned and disappeared into her bedroom a second time.

"Hugh will be hungry when he returns. I should get a start on our supper." She leaned the rifle in the corner. "Just as soon as I wash up." She headed for her bedroom. "Bandit, are you—"

The words died in her throat.

Her bedroom was in shambles. Sheets and blankets torn off the bed. Clothes pulled from her dresser and wardrobe. Books strewn across the floor. Her keepsake box upended, envelopes and other items scattered hither and yon.

Then her heart stopped.

The money box. It was on the floor, too, the lock broken, the lid open. Empty.

"O Lord," she whispered. "No."

She went to the metal box and picked it up. Her money gone. Taken. Why hadn't she hidden it better? Why hadn't she—

Hopelessness washed over her. Without that money, she was ruined. She couldn't pay her taxes. She would be forced to sell or lose it. Charlie would get the ranch, just as he'd told her he would. She sank onto the bed, tears pooling in her eyes.

"What do I do now?"

Bandit came to her and laid his muzzle on her knee. The dog's affectionate action caused Julia to cry in earnest, emitting soft sobs every so often while stroking Bandit's head.

Where was Hugh? She would feel better if he were with her. She wanted Hugh more than anything right now.

A sound from outside—a footfall on the porch —caused her to catch her breath once again.

"Mrs. Grace? Are you in there, ma'am?"

She released the breath. Lance Noonan's voice. "Yes, sheriff. I'm here. Just a moment." She swiped at her damp cheeks with her fingertips. The sheriff. Had God sent him in her time of need? Could he possibly find the thief before it was too late? She drew a deep breath, set the money box aside, and left her bedroom.

When the sheriff saw her, he removed his hat. "Afternoon, Mrs. Grace."

"Good afternoon."

"I'm sorry to bother you, but I . . . I had some disturbing information come across my desk a couple of days ago. I would've come to see you then, but I heard you were driving the cattle to the Double T."

239

"It sounds urgent, sheriff. What is it?"

"Is Mr. Brennan still working for you?"

"Hugh? Yes. Well, no. Not really. I hired him for the cattle drive. We got back yesterday, and he plans to leave on Monday." *Unless I can change his mind.*

"Is he around now so I could talk to him?"

"Not just now. Why?"

"Seems he's a thief, ma'am. Jewels and such. And he served time in an Illinois prison for attempted murder. Stabbed a man in the back during a robbery."

"I don't believe it." Even as the words came out of her mouth, she thought about the missing money and the disarray in her bedroom. Doubt bubbled to the surface. Where *was* Hugh?

"It's true, all right. I confirmed it myself."

She remembered Hugh, early that morning, standing almost exactly where the sheriff stood now. How he'd picked up Angus's mother's ring and told her it was worth more than the cattle she'd sold. It had seemed strange at the time that he should know a ring's value. And hadn't he watched her closely the day before, after she'd put the cash into the money box? Was it possible . . . ? No. No, she refused to believe it. It wasn't true. Hugh wouldn't steal from her.

A tiny sob escaped her throat.

"Mrs. Grace, are you sure everything's all right?"

"No, sheriff," she answered softly. "It isn't. I—"
She looked toward her bedroom. "I've been robbed."

"What was taken?"

"All the money from the sale of the cattle." She motioned for him to follow her. "I returned a short while ago to find this."

Sheriff Noonan stopped in her bedroom doorway, his gaze taking in the mess the thief had left behind. "Anything else missing besides the money?"

Julia started to shake her head, but uncertainty stopped her. She hadn't really looked after seeing the empty money box.

She knelt on the floor by the upended keepsake box. She retrieved the letters first and put them back where they belonged. Her grandmother's necklace peeked out at her from beneath her bedstead. A little more searching located the silver cross under her pillow on the floor.

But where was the ring? Angus's mother's ugly ring.

"Mrs. Grace?"

She looked up.

"Something else is missing." It wasn't a question this time.

She nodded. "A ring. But I . . . I don't know that it was worth anything much. It belonged to Angus's mother."

"Maybe you'd better tell me where I can find Mr. Brennan so he and I can have a talk."

Tears once again stung her eyes. "I don't know

where he is. I came back a short while ago and his horse was gone."

"Mind if I have a look at his bunk?"

"Of course not." She stood. "I'll show you where he stays."

Hugh didn't do this. He couldn't do this. I know he couldn't do it.

She repeated the words in her mind again and again as she left the house, crossed the yard, and entered the barn. She believed the words right up until the moment she opened the door to the room that held the bed, lantern, table, and chairs. But nothing else. All of Hugh's personal effects were gone. No saddlebags. No clothes hanging on hooks. No Bible.

From behind her, the sheriff said, "Looks like he decided to leave before Monday."

Julia found it hard to draw breath.

"Guess we know who took your money and ring."

She wanted to wail. She wanted to scream. She wanted to curl up and die.

"Love is a risk," Rose's voice whispered in her memory. *"But it's a risk worth taking."*

Her friend couldn't be more wrong. It wasn't worth the risk. Nothing could be worth the way Julia felt now. Nothing.

Hugh awakened with a start, heart racing. A nightmare? No, he hadn't been dreaming and he wasn't afraid.

He sat up and looked around. His horse stood, head low, near a tree. A nearly full moon illuminated his campsite. The air was filled with the sound of flowing water from the stream a stone's throw from Hugh's bed on the ground. The fire had burned down to embers.

Something had awakened him. Something like . . . like a whisper. Only not a whisper. There was no voice. There was no sound above the gurgle of the creek.

Go back.

The words weren't just in his head. They filled him to the brim. It was God's voice he heard. He knew it with more certainty than he'd ever known anything in his life.

Go back.

Julia needed him, and even if she didn't love him, even if she could never love him, he had to be there for her as long as she needed his help. Charlie Prescott could threaten Hugh all he wanted, and it wouldn't change his mind. He had to go back and help her. He wouldn't allow her brother-in-law to take what was rightfully hers.

And he couldn't wait for daylight to start back toward Sage-hen. Hugh tossed aside the blanket and reached for his boots.

Twenty-five

It was midmorning on one of those Sundays in June when the air is fresh and the sky seems extra blue. Normally, such a day would draw words of praise to God from Julia's lips as she sat by the river. But this morning, her heart felt numb. Too numb to read or write or sing or praise. Almost too numb to breathe. Too numb to keep on living. Not in the sort of way that made her want to throw herself into the river and drown. In the kind of way where a body could lay down and simply die for lack of a will to go on.

Such were her thoughts when Bandit alerted her to the approach of another. Her heart quickened a moment—was it Hugh?—before her hopes were dashed. The man on horseback wasn't Hugh. It was Charlie. Tired as she was, she got to her feet. She wouldn't allow him to tower over her more than necessary.

"Good morning, Julia." He stopped his horse and leaned a forearm on the pommel.

She acknowledged him with a nod.

"I heard about the robbery. Folks are talking about it in town."

"People shouldn't gossip."

"I wouldn't call it gossip. The sheriff was seeking more deputies to look for Mr. Brennan.

Naturally the word got out." He shook his head. "I knew that fellow was no good."

She hadn't the strength to deal with her brother-in-law. She wanted him to leave. This was still her land, at least for another nineteen days. "Did you want something, Charlie?"

"Yes. I want to help you."

Help her? He couldn't help her with what mattered most—her broken heart.

"Let me buy your ranch now, before you lose it over unpaid taxes. You can leave Sage-hen with money in your pocket. Isn't that better than being destitute?"

Even with her mind clouded by depression and her heart empty of hope, Julia knew Charlie would never offer such a thing for kindness's sake. Perhaps he wanted to look beneficent to his neighbors or to other men in places of power. Perhaps he wasn't willing to wait a few more months for the ranch to be auctioned off. Whatever his reasons, they didn't matter to her. Not now. She had lost something of much more value than this ranch, than land or livestock.

"I'm not going to sell," she said.

"Julia, be—"

"Please go away." She turned her back toward him.

There was a lengthy stretch of silence, then, "Angus always said you were both stubborn *and* stupid. I see he was right. Have it your way."

She waited until the sound of hoofbeats faded into nothing before she sank once more to the ground, surprised to find there were more tears left to be shed after all.

Hugh figured he was less than an hour outside of Pine Creek when he stopped to rest his horse. He sat on the ground in the shade of a tall tree to eat some beef jerky while the gelding grazed nearby. That's where he was when three men on horseback found him. One of them was the sheriff. A bad feeling washed over Hugh as he stood to meet them.

"Hugh Brennan?" the sheriff said, as if there might be some question about his identity even though they'd met before.

"Yes."

Sheriff Noonan bumped his hat brim with his knuckles. "Didn't expect to find you this close to town."

The words had an ominous ring to them.

"We need you to come back to Pine Creek with us."

Even more ominous. "What for?"

"Just need to ask you a few questions. About Mrs. Grace."

"Julia?" He forgot his own misgivings. "What about her? What's happened? Is she all right?"

"It'll be better if we talk about it back at my office."

Hugh went to his horse, took the reins in hand, and swung into the saddle. "Then let's go." He kicked the gelding in the ribs, and the horse shot forward.

The sheriff and his deputies were behind Hugh in an instant. Instinct told him that if he tried to get away, one of them would shoot him. But he had no intention of trying to get away. He had to know what happened to Julia—and getting to Pine Creek would put him that much closer to her.

Sheriff Noonan rode up beside him. "Slow down, Brennan. We aren't going to a fire."

Hugh recognized a command from a man of authority when he heard it. Years in prison had taught him that. He reined his horse back to a slow trot. Then he looked at the sheriff. "Has Mrs. Grace been hurt? Was there an accident at the ranch?"

"No. No accident. She's not hurt."

He felt some of the tension leave his shoulders. Whatever had sent these lawmen to find him, he could deal with it as long as he knew Julia was unharmed. They rode the rest of the way to town in silence, Hugh beside Lance Noonan, the two deputies following close behind them.

Based upon the number of families walking on the boardwalk in their Sunday best, church services in Pine Creek were over by the time the four men got to town. Some of those families paused to stare at the horsemen as they rode by.

Hugh had the feeling they knew something he didn't. It wasn't a good feeling.

In front of the jail, they dismounted and tied their mounts to the hitching post.

"Rogers," the sheriff said, "take care of Mr. Brennan's belongings."

"Yessir."

Hugh frowned.

"Come inside, Brennan."

Something happened to Hugh as he followed Sheriff Noonan into his office. First, dread washed over him and the walls seemed to close in. It was like being in one of his nightmares and not unexpected. But before panic could take hold, he felt gripped by a sudden stillness instead. Peace. As if he'd been plucked from the heart of a storm and was now above the wind. Unlike the dread, the latter feeling was most unexpected. It had to be the Lord's peace. There was no other explanation for it.

Hold fast. As in the night, the words seemed audible, although they weren't.

"Have a seat," the sheriff said as he walked to the opposite side of his desk and sat in his own chair.

One of the two deputies, Rogers, came into the office. He looked at the sheriff and gave his head a shake.

The sheriff cocked a brow, as if doubting the man.

"Nothing," Rogers said.

Lance Noonan looked at Hugh. "Mind showing me what's in your pockets."

It was obvious they suspected him of stealing something. Knowing it should have sent Hugh into a panic, but that strange, powerful, wonderful calm continued to blanket him as he stood and reached into his pants-pockets, withdrawing a pocketknife from one and the wages Julia had paid him from another. From his shirt pocket, he pulled a handkerchief. He put the items on the sheriff's desk.

"Is that it?"

"That's it."

The sheriff frowned. "Where were you headed, Brennan?"

"When you found me? Back to Sage-hen. Before that, I was on my way to Boise. Only I changed my mind about leaving just yet. And since I obviously don't have what you're looking for, maybe you should tell me what this is about and let me be on my way."

"Mrs. Grace was robbed."

His peace was momentarily shaken. "Was she hurt?"

"No. She wasn't home at the time."

"And you think I did it."

"Given your history—" Sheriff Noonan paused to make his point.

Hugh understood. Charlie Prescott knew about

his time in prison. The sheriff knew he'd been a thief. And now Julia knew the truth as well.

"Mrs. Grace came home to a house that was ransacked, her money box broken into, and you'd left without a word."

"I left her a note." It sounded even more cowardly coming out of his mouth than when he'd first thought about it yesterday.

"She didn't mention a note to me."

Hugh rubbed a hand over his face. If he were the sheriff of Pine Creek, he'd toss him into a cell and throw away the key—and yet the peace persisted. "Was anything else taken?"

"Only other thing missing besides the money was a ring."

The ring. The one Hugh had seen yesterday morning.

Guilty, a different voice whispered in his mind. An ugly voice. One meant to shake him.

Hold fast, came the words that kept him steady.

The office door opened, drawing Hugh's eyes to it. There in the doorway stood Peter Collins.

"Is it true?" Peter demanded, his gaze shifting to the sheriff. "You've arrested Hugh."

"No." The sheriff stood. "It isn't true. I had some questions for him, but he's not under arrest. Yet."

A look of relief passed over Peter's face. "Good, because I can tell you, you'd be making a mistake if you did arrest him. This man would never steal. And definitely not from Julia Grace."

A sick feeling twisted Hugh's gut. "Peter, I—"

"I've already heard the talk about your time in prison. But that's in your past. I know the man you are today, Hugh. The other's over and done with. I can take the measure of a man, and you're no thief, no matter what you once did or who you once were. I'd stake my life on it."

Waiting for her husband to come out of the sheriff's office, Rose sat on the wagon seat, Jemima sleeping in her arms, and prayed. She prayed that Peter would know what to say and do. She prayed that Hugh would be the man she and Peter thought him to be. She prayed that Julia's faith wouldn't be shaken. She prayed that the money would be found.

"When're we goin' home, Ma?" Eden asked from the wagon bed. "I'm gettin' hungry."

"Me too," Faith chimed in.

"I know, girls. Be patient. Your pa had something to do. We'll be on our way soon."

Lord, please work a miracle. I'm pretty sure it'll take one to clear up this mess.

The door to the sheriff's office opened. Peter stepped onto the boardwalk first. A moment later, Hugh Brennan appeared beside him. Both men set their hats on their heads as they looked her way.

"Pa," Eden called, "we're hungry. Can we go home now?"

"Sure can," Peter answered. Then he turned toward Hugh and offered his hand. "I don't suppose you'd care to ride along with us."

"No. I need to get to the ranch. I need to talk to Julia." Hugh took Peter's hand and shook it. "I appreciate all you said in there."

"Just spoke the truth."

Rose saw something flicker across Hugh's face. She couldn't say what it was for certain, only that it made her heart ache for him. The two men broke apart. Peter stepped down into the street and up onto the wagon seat. Hugh swung into the saddle.

"Mr. Brennan," Rose said quickly. "Tell Julia I'm praying for her."

He gave her a tight smile as he nodded. Then he turned his horse down Main Street and rode off.

Rose went straight back to praying.

Julia held a kitten between her hands and rubbed its soft fur against her cheek. She would need to ask Rose to give the cat and her litter a home. She couldn't bear to leave Sage-hen without knowing they would be taken care of.

How long after the taxes were due before the sheriff came to evict her? Days? Weeks? A few months? And where would she go when the time came?

"Julia?"

She sucked in a breath. His voice sounded so real. As if he were present instead of just in her head.

"Julia."

She whirled around.

Hugh stood in the barn doorway, the light at his back, his face hidden in shadows. But it was truly him and not a memory or wishful thinking. He was real and standing before her, and in that instant, she knew in her heart he hadn't betrayed her. No matter what he'd done or the reason he'd left, she believed in him.

She put the kitten back with its mother, then moved a few steps toward Hugh. "The sheriff's looking for you."

"I know. We spoke already."

"He didn't arrest you?"

"No." He shook his head.

She drew in a breath of relief.

"I didn't steal from you, Julia."

"I know. I thought you did, for a little while. But I don't believe it now."

"I tried to explain in the note."

"What note?"

Though she couldn't see it, she heard the frown in his voice. "The sheriff said you didn't mention one, but I left a note for you. I shouldn't have done it that way. I should have waited for you, told you the truth in person. I'm sorry."

"I didn't find a note. What did it say?"

"How I thought I was doing what was best for you, by leaving. I thought it was best for me too."

"And I thought you were gone for good."

"But I was wrong. So I turned around and came back."

A smile slipped into place on her lips. "You came back." The sheriff hadn't brought him back. He'd come of his own accord. Something warm and wonderful wrapped around her heart.

"Yes." It was his turn to take a couple of steps forward. "I need to tell you about my past. About the things I did and why I . . . why I went to prison."

"Later. Tell me later. After supper."

"I want you to know everything. No secrets between us. Not any. Just the truth."

Throat tight, she nodded.

"I love you, Julia." Another step closer. "You may not want my love, especially after you know what I used to be, but you at least need to know how I feel about you."

She could see his face clearly now. The faint scar on his right cheek. The lines around his brown eyes and his mouth. The dark stubble that said he hadn't shaved that morning.

He loved her. He'd returned because he loved her.

"I don't have much of anything to offer you, Julia. I don't have any money except what you paid me to work for you. I've got a good horse and saddle, a Winchester rifle, and a Bible. I've got a strong back, and I'm willing to work hard."

"When I lose the ranch, I won't have much more than that myself."

"Maybe you won't lose it. Maybe the sheriff can find who took the money and get it back."

"Maybe." She didn't believe it for an instant—and it didn't matter, now that Hugh was with her again. The idea of leaving Sage-hen no longer frightened her. Not as long as she was with him.

He took another step closer. "Julia Grace, I think it's time I kissed you."

Past time. A surprise, to want a man's kisses. But she wanted his.

He gathered her close and lowered his head. The first touch of his lips upon hers sent unexpected sensations coursing through her. Startled, she drew back and looked at him, wide-eyed. He let her stay there only a moment before tightening his hold and kissing her again.

How was it possible she'd reached her age—almost thirty!—and been married eleven years and conceived three babies and still never knew a kiss could make her feel like this? Shaken but strong. Shattered but soaring. Lovable and loved.

Hugh gently gripped her upper arms while taking a step back from her. He cleared his throat. "I . . . uh . . . I'd better take care of my horse."

His voice was low and tense. Passion smoldered in his eyes.

She saw it and wasn't afraid. She wasn't afraid because with the passion she recognized his control of it.

I love you too, she wanted to tell him, but the words remained lodged in her throat. The last time she'd shared those feelings with anyone, she'd been a child telling her mother. Since then, only God had heard of her devotion. Now it seemed that she didn't know how to give voice to that emotion, even when she wanted to.

They sat in the parlor after supper, Julia in one chair, Hugh in the other, and he told her his story. About his childhood in the tenements of Chicago. About his father's drinking and his frequent and lengthy absences. About his mother's death. About his experiences on the train with the other orphans from Dr. Cray's Asylum for Little Wanderers. About his father coming for him in Nebraska and their return to Chicago. About his introduction into a life of crime, picking pockets, slipping into homes through open windows. About the night his father stabbed a man who surprised them in the middle of a robbery and how he left Hugh to be arrested for attempted murder. About the quick trial and the long, hard years in prison. About everything that had eventually brought him into the barnyard at Sage-hen.

She listened with scarcely a change in expression.

Hugh couldn't remember another time in his life when he had been as honest with anyone, not even his mum. It was hard to ignore the niggle of fear he felt, laying his life bare before this woman he'd come to adore. She might reject him, now that she knew the truth. She might send him away. He couldn't blame her if she did.

But rather than demanding he clear out, that he put his few things back into the saddlebags and ride off, she told him her story. Some of it—the parts about her husband's abuse—he'd suspected before now from little things she'd said, from certain looks in her eyes. Some of it—the part about her stillborn babies and the miscarriage— he'd guessed from the small graves on a knoll. But the stories of her childhood in the mining town and her mother's occupation and how Julia had come to marry Angus Grace, those he couldn't have guessed.

Gloaming had fallen over the earth by the time she finished. Crickets took up an evening song, the sounds drifting through the open front door along with a fresh breeze. Softly, Julia said, " 'And I will restore to you the years that the locust hath eaten.' "

Hugh didn't know the verse, but he knew her words must be from Scripture.

She smiled sadly. "It's a promise from God that

I've held onto through the years. When nothing else makes sense to me, I cling to Him and to that promise from His Word."

He'd told her he loved her. He'd also told her he had nothing to give her. His pockets were empty. Hadn't her life been difficult enough? Could he invite her to share his poverty? Was it wrong of him to even consider it? He didn't want her to go with him only because she'd lost this place. He wanted her to have a choice. She'd had few enough of those in her life. Something he hadn't understood before. He wanted to do everything in his power to give her that choice.

He stood. "I think I'll turn in. Been a long day."

"Yes." She stood too. Confusion swirled in her eyes.

Although he wanted to take her back into his arms, to hold her, to shelter her, to kiss her, to love her, he didn't. Although he hoped she would tell him she loved him, she didn't.

He touched her cheek with his fingertips. "We'll figure out something, Julia. I promise. We'll figure out a way for you to keep the ranch."

Twenty-six

In that moment between dreams and reality, between sleep and wakefulness, Julia envisioned her arms outstretched, her hands turned palms up but tightly clenched. Then she pictured the Lord gently trying to loosen her fists.

Let go, beloved. There isn't anything you can hang onto that I'm not wanting to replace with something far better. Let go and receive.

Letting go of Sage-hen meant she could grab hold of Hugh. She could go with him wherever he wanted and be all right. Security was found only in God, and her home would be found only with Hugh.

As a smile played across her mouth, she envisioned her hands again, empty and open and ready to receive.

Before the sun was up, Julia rode to the knoll where her babies were buried. She took with her some wildflowers she'd found growing near the house. Kneeling beneath the gnarled tree, she placed the flowers on the ground, then touched the small headstones with her gloved fingertips, first one, then the other. She'd never had a chance to know them, but she loved them as if she had. She wouldn't love them less or miss them less if she didn't live on this ranch.

"I will take you with me in my heart wherever I go," she said softly.

The sound of cantering hoofbeats caused her to look up. She wasn't surprised to see Hugh riding toward her. In fact, she realized she'd been expecting him to come to find her.

Love blossomed in her chest, a feeling so strong, so sweet, so all-encompassing that she could scarcely draw breath. She'd thought she would never love or be loved, that she could never entrust her body or soul into another man's care. But she loved Hugh. She trusted him. She believed in him. When God brought him to Sage-hen, He had changed her mourning into joy, her ashes into something beautiful, and the heaviness of her spirit into songs of praise.

She stood, putting a hand above her eyes to shield them from the rising sun. "You found me."

"I thought this was where you'd be after our talk last night." He dismounted.

"I was saying goodbye."

"There's still time. We might figure out a way to—"

"You don't understand, Hugh." She took two steps toward him. "It isn't Sage-hen I want." *God, give me the words to say to make him understand.* The prayer had no more than formed in her mind before she had her answer—and the boldness to speak the words aloud. " 'Intreat me not to leave thee, or to return from following after thee: for whither thou goest, I will go; and where thou lodgest, I will lodge: thy people shall be my people, and thy God my God: where thou diest, will I die, and there will I be buried: the Lord do so to me, and more also, if ought but death part thee and me.' "

Conflicting emotions played across his handsome face before he asked, "Are you sure, Julia?"

She nodded, her throat suddenly tight.

"It isn't because you have no other choice?"

"No, that isn't the reason." She drew a deep breath, ready at last to say the words aloud. "It's because I love you." She was in his arms before she realized he'd reached for her.

"Say it again."

"I love you, Hugh. With everything that I am, I love you."

She'd been disappointed last night when he'd returned to the barn without kissing her again. He made up for it now.

When at last he drew back, he said, "Will you marry me?"

She laughed, feeling giddy. "Of course."

"You're sure? I know you—"

"I'm sure."

God could strike Hugh dead right then and there, and he would arrive in heaven the happiest man who'd ever lived. Grace. Undeserved favor.

It had been poured out upon him most abundantly, but never in any manner more beautiful than the woman who wore the last name of Grace. Although she wouldn't wear it for long, if it was up to him.

Still smiling up at him, she said, "We must tell Rose and Peter and the girls."

"Do you think they'll be glad?"

"They'll be glad. Rose is the one who told me not to be afraid to love you."

"Remind me to thank her when we see her."

"Let's go now."

"Now? It's still mighty early. Don't you think we should give them time to eat breakfast first?"

"No." She laughed again.

He knew it then. He was in trouble. Deep trouble. He would never want to deny her anything. That was clear as day to him. Also clear was that he didn't care.

"All right. Whatever you want." He swept her feet off the ground and carried her toward the black gelding. "We'll go now."

Peter was walking out of the barn, carrying a bucket of fresh milk in his right hand, when he saw Julia and Hugh riding toward the farm, Bandit running out ahead of them. He stopped in the middle of the barnyard and awaited their arrival. He couldn't be sure what brought them to the house this early in the day, but he thought it a good sign that they were coming together.

When the horses and riders slowed to a walk, Peter said, "You're out mighty early."

"We have news." Julia seemed to glow from the inside out.

"From the look of you, must be good news." Peter jerked his head toward the house. "Let's go inside. Whatever it is, Rose will want to hear it firsthand." He shifted his gaze to Hugh. Maybe he wasn't glowing like Julia, but there was something about the way he sat in the saddle that made him look taller, stronger, more confident than he'd appeared the day before. If Peter was a gambling man, he'd wager he knew what those two had come here to say.

He led the way into the house.

The kitchen was in its usual state of morning commotion. The children were eating, talking, and laughing. Rose stood at the stove, stirring some-thing in a pan with her right hand while holding the baby against her hip with her left arm. When she glanced toward the table, she saw him walking toward her. "Oh, good. Peter, you're here. Put the milk down and take the baby while I—"

"We've got company, Rose."

"Company?" She pulled the pan off the stove before turning around. "Julia?" Her expression grew worried. "What's wrong? What's happened now?"

Julia's smile broadened. "Nothing bad."

"Thank God. I don't think I could stand more bad news."

"Here." Peter held out his arms while subduing a chuckle. It amazed him that she hadn't already guessed what was happening. "I'll take Jem."

His wife passed the baby to him, then wiped her hands on her apron. "Well?"

Julia turned toward Hugh who hadn't entered the kitchen yet. Reaching out to him, she drew him close to her side. "We came to tell you we're going to be married."

Rose's eyes widened. "Truly? I thought it would happen but I never expected it so soon." She hurried across the kitchen and embraced her friend. "I'm so happy for you." Hugh was the next to receive a hug. "So very happy."

Peter waited until his wife had released Hugh before he went over to offer his own—but more subdued—congratulations. He shook Hugh's hand and kissed Julia's cheek and wished them both much happiness.

"When will you marry?" Rose asked as she took the baby once again into her own arms.

Color rose in Julia's cheeks. "Soon. Very soon. This week maybe. At least before we leave for Boise."

Tears welled in Rose's eyes. "You're leaving so soon?"

Peter heard her rising anxiety. Her dread of what would happen if Charlie Prescott took over Sage-hen was palpable.

"Peter," Julia said, drawing his attention back to the moment. "We . . . Hugh and I . . . we were talking on the way over here. I've decided to ask the Trents if they'll buy the rest of my herd while the ranch is still mine. If not we can ship them to market and get whatever we can for them. We've got until the end of the month to sell them. That'll give me enough to pay the taxes this year, and I can leave Wyoming with a clean conscience, not owing anybody anything."

He nodded, surprised by her decision and yet not surprised.

"It would give me a year to find a buyer for Sage-hen before the taxes are due again."

"Charlie Prescott wants the land," Peter said, stating the obvious. "He'll buy it from you right now."

Julia looked at Rose. "I won't sell the ranch to Charlie, no matter what he offers."

"But—," Rose began.

"I won't sell to him, Rose. If the county takes the ranch next year, maybe he'll get it, but he won't get it from me." She turned her gaze to Peter again. "The laying hens I'll give to you, and I've got a cat with a litter of kittens I hope you'll take."

"Sure."

"And the horses, if you want them. All but Teddy, of course, and one we'll take with us as a packhorse."

"Afraid I couldn't pay you what they're worth."

Julia reached out and touched the back of his hand. "I don't want any money for them, Peter. Not from you. After all you and Rose have done for me through the years. It's enough to know you'll care for them."

Peter heard his wife sniff, and an unwelcome lump of emotion formed in his own throat.

"I'll sell what household goods we can't take with us," Julia continued. "Which means most everything. But if there's anything either of you want . . ."

It sounded to Peter as if she was fighting tears as well. If both women got to crying, they'd be drowning in saltwater in no time.

Two hours later, Julia kissed Rose's cheek as she hugged her, then said, "The Lord knew I wasn't meant to stay here for good. He brought Hugh to Sage-hen so I might go with him. I've never been so sure of anything in my life."

"I know. I see it in your eyes and I hear it in your voice. Was a time I hoped you might feel that way for my brother."

"I know."

Rose shook her head and offered a small smile. "Wasn't meant to be."

"No."

"Hugh's a good man. I can rest knowing he'll be looking out for you."

Julia nodded.

"You come tell us straightaway when you know the day of your wedding. We'll all want to be there."

"We will." Julia stepped off the porch and walked to her horse.

Hugh was already in the saddle. "Ready?"

In her mind, she saw her open hands once again and knew that God was filling them with something better than she could have known to ask for.

"I'm ready."

Twenty-seven

"I'm not sure this is a good idea after all," Hugh said as he tightened the cinch on his horse's saddle. "Not this soon. What if the thief comes back?" He turned to look at Julia. "I don't like the idea of you being here alone."

She rose on tiptoe and kissed his cheek, still surprised how much she loved having the right to do so. "The thief won't be back. He has everything of value already."

"I still wish—"

"Go on, Hugh. The sooner you start for the Double T, the sooner you'll have an answer from the Trents about the cattle and can come back."

One corner of his mouth rose in a wry grin. "Will you always be this stubborn?"

"I'm afraid so. It's the new, more opinionated me."

Hugh stepped into the saddle. "Guess I'd better get used to her."

She marveled at the pleasure that bubbled up inside over their silly banter.

"I'll be back tomorrow night," he said, the smile gone, his gaze both loving and intense.

"I'll watch for you."

As he rode away, she remembered the day—not so very long ago—that she'd sat astride Teddy, watching a train in the distance as it churned its way west. She'd wondered where its passengers were headed, what were their final destinations. Soon it would be Julia who would head west. First to Boise City. But then where? What would be their final destination, Julia and Hugh? She didn't know. She didn't think he knew either. Once the uncertainty of her future would have filled her with fear. No more.

She flicked her braid over her shoulder and tilted her chin upward, in defiance of her old insecurities. There was much to do before Hugh returned from the Trent ranch. She must decide what would be sold and what she would give to others and what she wanted to take with her. She must go into Pine Creek to see Reverend Peabody.

And she needed to tell Mrs. Humphrey at the mercantile that she would need a little more time before she paid her bill. Julia didn't doubt that the Trents would buy the remainder of her cattle, but she couldn't be certain how soon they would conclude the transaction.

Knowing she must tell Mrs. Humphrey that she couldn't pay her bill as yet helped Julia decide what she must do first. She would go to town. She would go now.

It took Hugh all the self-discipline he possessed not to push his horse too hard as he rode south and east, dropping down onto the vast Wyoming plains and finally following the railroad tracks toward the Double T Ranch. As the sounds of hoofbeats filled his ears, thoughts of Julia filled his mind, and he was surprised once again at what God had accomplished since he'd left Illinois in search of his sisters. On the trail he'd found salvation, redemption, forgiveness, and love.

Love.

He'd thought himself unworthy of a woman like Julia. He *was* unworthy of a woman like Julia. And yet she loved him despite all the reasons she shouldn't. Even after he'd told her the whole unvarnished truth, she still loved him. How had he thought, even for a short time, that he could ride away and never see her again? Knowing her, being with her, loving her made him whole in a place he hadn't known he was broken.

He couldn't get to the Double T and back to Sage-hen fast enough to suit him.

As Julia drew near to Pine Creek a couple of hours later, her thoughts remained on Hugh. She tried to imagine where he was by now. He would make good time without a bunch of obstinate cows to keep track of, but she wasn't familiar enough with the trail to guess how much ground he might have covered already.

Hurry there, Hugh. Hurry there and hurry back.

Her gelding crested a rise in the road and the town came into view. She called to Bandit and commanded him to stay close even as she slowed Teddy from a canter to a trot. When they reached the first building on the edge of Pine Creek, she reined the horse to a walk and guided him down Main Street toward the mercantile.

This would be one of her last visits to the town, she realized, and although the circumstances of her marriage to Angus had kept her mostly a stranger to its townsfolk and the townsfolk to her, she would miss those she knew when she was gone. Had circumstances been different . . .

She shook her head, casting off the doubt that tried to surface. Instead, she would embrace the future God had set before her.

After tethering Teddy to the hitching post, Julia went into the store. A quick glance around confirmed that she was the only customer at the moment. She was grateful for that. She didn't want everyone to know her business, good or bad.

Nancy Humphrey walked out of a back room. Her eyes widened when she saw Julia standing at the counter. "Why, Mrs. Grace. I didn't expect to see you."

"I needed to speak with you about my bill."

"You don't have to say a word. I know about the robbery. I'm so very sorry this happened."

"You will be paid, Mrs. Humphrey. I'm going to sell—"

The mercantile door opened and then closed with a bang.

"Nancy, have you heard?" a woman asked.

Julia looked behind her to see Marjorie O'Donnell hurrying down the aisle.

"Heard what?"

"The sheriff has arrested Charlie Prescott and Bryce Smith and the Waters brothers and Hank Gale."

"Good heavens! Whatever for?"

"Mr. Prescott bribed those men on the land board. That's why the taxes went up so high. It was supposed to drive folks out and then Mr. Prescott would buy the land for a song. It was all arranged. And Mr. Prescott had some sort of dishonest dealings going on with Mr. Smith at the bank too. I'm not sure exactly. Calling in mortgages or something like that. Oh, it's quite

271

the scandal, I tell you. Quite the scandal. I heard there is a federal agent in town. To think. Men of such standing would do such awful things to their neighbors, and now they'll be going to jail. There's to be an emergency meeting of the land board to elect new members, and I heard talk they'll be rescinding the increase in taxes. Glory be!"

Julia and Nancy exchanged looks.

If what Marjorie said was true, Rose had been right about Charlie all along. Her friend had said Charlie was more like Angus than Julia realized. Still, he'd been her brother-in-law for many years. The only family she'd had left after Angus died.

"And you are generous to him to a fault," Rose's voice whispered in her memory.

"Mrs. Humphrey," Julia said, "I will be back in a little while to speak to you."

She didn't wait for a response but turned, hurried out of the mercantile, and walked toward the sheriff's office. There was a group of men standing on the boardwalk not far from the jail's entrance, talking and speculating. Probably as they'd done when Sheriff Noonan had questioned Hugh on Sunday. When they saw her, they parted to let her pass.

She opened the door, half expecting to see Charlie sitting before the sheriff's desk, preparing to be sent home. But he wasn't there. He was in one of the cells, sitting on a cot, elbows braced on knees, holding his head in his hands.

Lance Noonan rose from his desk chair. "Mrs. Grace."

Charlie looked up.

"I was going to ride out to see you," the sheriff continued.

"I was at the mercantile and heard about the arrest."

"Yes, ma'am." He opened the drawer and withdrew something. "I believe this is yours." He held up his hand. Clasped between thumb and index finger was Angus's mother's missing ring.

"Where did you find it?" But she knew the answer before he could speak it.

"Mr. Prescott had it."

Julia turned and walked to the cell.

Charlie glowered at her as he stood.

"*You* broke into my house and stole my money? *You* took the ring?"

He didn't answer.

"I know you wanted Sage-hen, but was it worth going to jail?"

"I won't be in here long. My lawyers will get the charges thrown out." He sent an angry look in the direction of the sheriff. "He won't be able to hold me."

"I pity you, Charlie," she said softly.

"Pity me?" His eyes narrowed as his gaze returned to her.

"Your brother's ranch wouldn't satisfy you if you got it. You'd want more after that and more after that. Others were right about you. You're a man without love and without God. You're more like Angus than I thought you were."

He called her a vile name as he grabbed the bars of the cell. "You have no right to that ranch or that ring or anything else that belonged to my brother. Angus never loved you. He regretted the day he married you and brought you here to live. You were worthless to him. You couldn't even give him a child."

She waited to feel the familiar pain, but it didn't come. Memories of Angus could no longer hurt her. Charlie's words could no longer hurt her. She was free of them. The last time she'd seen her brother-in-law, she'd been a woman bereft of hope, but that was no longer true of her. Now she was a woman who was loved and wanted and valued as she'd never been before. Not just by Hugh. Not just by her friends. But by God. She was a woman who had opened her hands to receive from the Lord, and He was filling them to overflowing.

"Perhaps that's all true, Charlie, but I am worth something to others." She took a step backward. "I'm worth something to God. I will endeavor to pray for you from time to time, that God may have His way with you." She turned and walked back to the sheriff's desk.

He said, "I can't let you have the ring yet, Mrs. Grace. It's evidence. But it will be returned eventually."

"Can you tell me, is it true that the increase in taxes will be rescinded?"

"I imagine so since the vote was illegal."

Her thoughts churned. Wait until she could tell Hugh what happened in his absence. Perhaps they could stay at Sage-hen. Perhaps they wouldn't have to sell the last of the cattle. Perhaps they—

The words swirling in her head quieted, and she knew that they wouldn't be staying on the ranch or in Wyoming. God had another place and another purpose for them. She knew it with every fiber of her being. And she was content.

Twenty-eight

Late on Friday morning, Hugh stood in the parlor of Julia's house, waiting for his bride to appear in the doorway of her bedroom. With him were Reverend Peabody, Peter, and the entire Collins brood, save for Rose. She was in the bedroom with Julia.

"Breathe, my friend," Peter whispered, laughter in his voice.

Hugh glanced to his right. "I thought I *was* breathing."

"Didn't look like it." Peter's grin widened. "I

was nervous on my wedding day too. It's normal."

Peter was wrong about the nervous part. Hugh wasn't nervous. Not about marrying Julia. There wasn't a doubt in his mind that God had brought him to Sage-hen for this purpose. He'd been pondering that realization all week. Here on this ranch, with Julia, the Lord had completed a work begun on the plains of eastern Colorado. He'd set Hugh free from the sins of his past. He'd opened up a new and better future for him than he could have imagined for himself when he left Illinois. That's what had him unconsciously holding his breath—amazement over what Christ had done for him when he learned to trust Him completely and submit to Him totally. And He'd done the same for Julia.

The bedroom door opened at last. Rose came out first, but Hugh scarcely noticed her once his bride stepped into view. She wore a blue dress the exact same color as her eyes. Except for a broach near her collar, the gown was unadorned. Her hair had been swept upward and decorated with tiny blue flowers.

He'd never seen anything or anyone more beautiful in all his life.

She came toward him, a small smile on her lips.

Another reason for amazement. Considering the kind of life she'd endured with Angus, no one could have blamed her if she'd chosen never to

marry again. But she *had* chosen to marry again
. . . and she'd chosen to marry Hugh. A miracle if
ever there was one.

He held out his hand and drew her to his side,
returning her smile.

"Very good," the reverend said. "Shall we begin?"

For the briefest of moments, Julia remembered
her first wedding, the bride seventeen and shy
and uncertain and hopeful and frightened. But
looking into Hugh's eyes cast out the memory.

"Dearly beloved . . ."

In a short while she would be married to Hugh
Brennan. In a matter of weeks, they would ride
away from Sage-hen for good to begin a new life
elsewhere. Where once such a thought would
have filled her with fear, now she felt a peace
and comfort. Perhaps even some excitement.

*The locust ate so many years, Lord, but look
at Your restoration.*

She smiled again, and her groom smiled at her
in return. A flutter of anticipation erupted in her
midsection. It seemed as if she had been awaiting
this day her entire life. That every other experience in her life had been leading her to this one.
The joy she felt was indescribable.

When the minister asked them to repeat their
vows, she gladly did so in her turn. When he
pronounced them man and wife, she gladly kissed
her new husband in front of their witnesses.

When Peter toasted their happiness, she gladly sipped the punch Rose had made. And when their guests and the Reverend Peabody bid them farewell, she gladly stood on the porch, Hugh at her side with his arm around her waist, and waved goodbye to them all.

And then they were alone, just the two of them. Mr. and Mrs. Hugh Brennan.

Silence fell around them, and with it came a sense of the sacred, a new understanding of the beauty of marriage in the eyes of God. Hugh turned her toward him and held her close as he kissed her, explored her mouth with his own, unhurried, tender, loving.

And she was not afraid.

Julia was alone in the bed when she awakened. From the light filtering through the window curtains, she saw that afternoon had drifted into evening while she napped. Her stomach growled, reminding her how long it had been since she'd eaten anything. Not since breakfast, and that had been slight because of her wedding preparations. Perhaps if she waited here in bed, her husband would return to the bedroom with a tray of food.

My husband.

Even loving Hugh as she did, she hadn't expected to feel this way, knowing he was hers and she was his. She hadn't expected to delight in the little ways he understood her. She loved how he could tease her with a smile. She loved the passion of his kisses. She loved the tenderness in his touch.

She stretched, arms above her head, and was tempted to purr like a cat. Was it possible to be this happy?

"Oh, I am being silly," she said to herself as she reached for her robe.

Out of bed, she walked barefoot to the parlor. Hugh wasn't there nor was he in the kitchen. She went to the front door and looked outside in time to see him walking toward the house, milk pail in hand, Bandit following at his side.

She smiled, remembering the way the dog used to warily observe Hugh, even growl at him. "Bandit," she called, "have you forgotten he called you mangy?"

Hugh looked up with a grin. "You're awake at last."

A flush of pleasure rose to burn her cheeks.

He opened his mouth to say something, but the sound of hoofbeats interrupted him. They both looked toward the road leading to the house. It was Rose, alone in the surrey, which she seldom used because she usually had the children with her.

If it had been anyone else, Julia would have slipped back into the house to put on something more appropriate for this hour of the day. She would have done something with her hair too. But this was Rose, and she wouldn't have returned to Sage-hen today—Julia's wedding day —if something urgent hadn't sent her.

Could it have to do with Charlie? Was he out of jail as he'd promised he would be?

Julia stepped to the edge of the porch, tightening the tie around her waist as she did so.

"Julia!" Rose waved something in her hand. "Julia, you got a letter from your mother."

She reached for the nearby post to steady her suddenly weak legs.

Rose climbed out of the surrey and hurried to the porch steps. "Peter went into town, and Mrs. O'Donnell asked if he would deliver this to you. She knew you'd be anxious to receive it."

Anxious hardly described Julia's feelings. She hadn't expected an answer, after all. Her mother had sent back her letters for so long without reading them. Why had she read this one? Why had she taken the time to respond? Perhaps Julia's silence of the past three years had made her mother curious.

She took the letter from Rose's outstretched hand, then lifted her gaze to meet Hugh's. She read the concern in his eyes.

"Go inside and read it," Rose said. "You don't need an audience."

Not having words to respond, she could only do as her friend instructed. She went into the house and sank onto a chair in the parlor. Holding the envelope between both hands, she stared at the return address: *Madeline Crane, Grand Coeur, Idaho.* She ran her right index finger over the writing. Finally, she turned the envelope over, broke the seal, and removed the stationery inside.

Dearest Julia,

There is no way I could explain my feelings when I saw your name on the envelope carrying your letter. I thought I would never hear from you again. I thought your anger toward me was final and that you were ignoring the letters I sent to you.

My dear daughter, I never returned any letters to you unopened. I promise you, that is true. I would not think of doing so, not when I have been so hungry for word from you.

I cannot say that I am sorry for Angus Grace's death, knowing how he hurt you. Nor can I forgive myself for the part I played in putting you in that situation. Though I acted out of love, I made a horrid mistake. How foolish I was. How careless with the one person in my life I held so dear.

You asked if I am still with Madame Rousseau. No, I no longer work for her. I have a little business of my own. It was left to me, several years ago, in the will of a man who wished to marry me. I cannot claim that I am accepted by the more respectable folks in Grand Coeur, but I am no longer looked at the way I once was. You will be surprised to know that I even attend church services on occasion.

Please write to me again soon. I long to know more of your life.

With love,
Your devoted Mother

The final words on the page swam before Julia's tear-filled eyes. *With love . . .*

Letters sent and never received.

Letters never returned unopened.

How could this be?

She rose from the chair and walked into the bedroom. Once again, she retrieved her box of keepsakes from the wardrobe and took it with her to the bed where she sat. Opening the lid, she stared at the two bundles of letters. It was the bundle addressed to her mother that she withdrew. She untied the yellow ribbon and fanned the envelopes across her lap. "RETURNED TO WRITER" had been written across the front of each one, big and bold.

Angus's handwriting. Why hadn't she realized it before? Angus had never mailed her letters. He had wanted Julia to be cut off for good from her mother. Had he known what was in that last letter her mother received?

"Julia?"

She looked toward the sound of Hugh's voice. He stood in the bedroom doorway, clearly uncertain whether he should enter or not.

"Come in," she said softly, touching the mattress beside her.

He joined her there.

"Angus never mailed the letters. He made me believe my mother returned them to me instead. He must have intercepted the letters she sent to me too." She looked into his eyes. "How could anyone be that cruel?"

Hugh shook his head.

A tiny sob of joy escaped her. "She never stopped loving me."

He gathered her close, pressing his face into her hair, murmuring indistinct words of comfort. The keepsake box slid off the bed and hit the floor, but neither of them paid it any mind.

Twenty-nine

It was a blistering hot day in early July when Julia Brennan and Peter Collins sat in the two chairs near the desk, their respective spouses standing right behind them. On the other side of the desk was Roland March, attorney-at-law. Rose's brother had returned to Pine Creek in order to oversee the drafting and signing of the contract.

Just before Julia put pen to paper, she paused to

thank God once again. For the new life He'd given her. For the once tired and hungry stranger who had asked for a drink of water and a place to stay while his lame horse rested, the man who had shown her what love should be between a man and a woman. For the ways He'd provided for her, little ways and big ways, ordinary ways and miraculous ways. For the lessons of freedom and security, trust and surrender that she'd learned beneath His grace-filled tutelage. For the ability to know and follow His voice.

Today, she and Hugh would leave Pine Creek. They wouldn't leave wealthy. The sale of the cattle to the Trents had paid the taxes and Julia's debt at the mercantile and would give them enough to get settled wherever God led them. And when the trial was over, there would be the ring to sell, a ring as valuable as it was ugly. How amazing that God had provided for her in this way. As for Sage-hen Ranch, it was about to become the property of Peter and Rose Collins with a non-interest-bearing contract and reasonable annual payments to begin next year.

Roland cleared his throat. "Mrs. Brennan? Are you ready to sign?"

"Yes." With a nod, she drew in her wandering thoughts and looked at Peter. "But I believe I need to see the down payment first."

He grinned as he fulfilled her request, putting the money onto the desk and sliding it toward her.

She looked at it, then glanced over her shoulder at Hugh who nodded. Laughing softly, she signed her name to the contract, transferring ownership of Sage-hen Ranch from Julia Grace Brennan to Peter and Rose Collins for a down payment of one dollar.

Julia couldn't help believing herself the richest woman on the face of the earth.

Epilogue

September 1899, Frenchman's Bluff, Idaho

Hugh leaned a shoulder against the doorjamb, watching as adults and children ate birthday cake and drank punch at a long table set up in the yard behind the mercantile. They were all there to celebrate the eleventh birthday of Charity Murphy, Hugh's niece by marriage. His sister, Felicia Murphy, sat at one end of the table, cradling her three-month-old son in the crook of her left arm, while her husband, Colin, stood at the other end of the table, serving second slices of birthday cake to those who wanted it. There were a half dozen other kids close to Charity's age, along with some of their parents, filling up the benches on either side of the table. Laughter and chatter flooded the late summer air.

It surprised Hugh how quickly he and Julia

had become a part of the community of Frenchman's Bluff after their arrival in late July. He'd gone to work on one of the ranches outside of town, and Julia had set up housekeeping in the cottage behind the mercantile. He thought it likely they would put down roots in this small town, make a home, God willing, even start a family. Goodness knows, Julia's mother was hopeful for a grand-child to spoil. On their visit to Grand Coeur last month, Madeline had said she was considering selling her shop and moving to Boise City so she would be close when a baby came. He'd been afraid such talk would sadden Julia, remind her of the babies she'd lost. But instead, her eyes had alighted with joy, as if hearing her mother's words had given her permission to hope once again for a child.

His sister looked in his direction, smiled, and waved. He grinned and waved back.

That was another thing that surprised Hugh. The deep bond he'd felt with Felicia from the first moment they were reunited. In some ways, it was as if they'd never been apart.

The only way the party scene before him could be better was if their little sister, Diana, was there too. Felicia hadn't been all that hard to find once he'd started looking. But Diana? It looked as if that might not be as easy. All of his attempts so far had met with dead ends.

From behind him came Julia's soft voice.

"Why are you standing here by yourself? Don't you want some cake?"

Wordlessly, he reached for her, drawing her to his side.

"You're thinking about Diana, aren't you?"

He chuckled. "How did you do that?"

"Do what?"

"Read my mind."

"It isn't your mind I read, Hugh," she answered, love woven into her words. "It's your heart."

He lowered his head and kissed her on the lips.

He didn't suppose life would always be rosy. He knew difficult times would come. Rain fell on the just and unjust, like the Good Book said. Maybe they wouldn't be able to have children, no matter how much they were wanted. Maybe he wouldn't be able to find Diana and have his whole family together again. But whatever happened or didn't happen, God would be with them. The Lord would make the path clear before them and see them through.

Life was sometimes hard.

God was always good.

On that they could depend.

Center Point Large Print
600 Brooks Road / PO Box 1
Thorndike ME 04986-0001 USA

(207) 568-3717

US & Canada:
1 800 929-9108
www.centerpointlargeprint.com